Florence Dixie

Redeemed in Blood

Volume 2

Florence Dixie

Redeemed in Blood
Volume 2

ISBN/EAN: 9783337392222

Printed in Europe, USA, Canada, Australia, Japan

Cover: Foto ©Andreas Hilbeck / pixelio.de

More available books at **www.hansebooks.com**

BY

LADY FLORENCE DIXIE,

Author of " Abel Avenged," "Waifs and Strays," " Across Patagonia,"
"In the Land of Misfortune," " The Young Castaways," etc.

IN THREE VOLUMES.

VOL. II.

LONDON:

HENRY AND COMPANY,

6, BOUVERIE STREET, E.C.

1889.

Printed by Hazell, Watson, & Viney, Ld., London and Aylesbury.

REDEEMED IN BLOOD.

CHAPTER XI.

IT was midday. The sky above was of a deep azure-blue; the sun shone forth upon its sapphire shade, reflecting in the glassy waters beneath a scene of exquisite loveliness. There was a hum of insects all around; the heat was intense; scarce a breeze from the distant sea crept in upon the stilly air. A haze floated like a crystal veil along the tropical girt hills that rose up on either side of the land-locked bay of the grandest harbour in the world; for the scene we are describing is Rio Harbour.

Ships of war dotted that vast bay; craft of every kind and nationality rode at anchor therein; little boats plied to and fro between them and the shore, busy bearing fruits or provisions to their holds. And from amidst the wealth of green, whose mantle clothed the rising slopes on either side, showed forth conspicuously the white and yellow houses of those who lived away from the town of Rio itself.

Anchored in solitary grandeur, and conspicuous by its huge size and marked isolation, a mighty ironclad lay riding the placid waters of Rio Harbour. A small boat coming from the shore might have been seen approaching this monarch of the deep, and standing watching its approach from the upper deck of H.M.S. *Bucephalus*—for so the great war-vessel was named—were two smart young midshipmen.

One of them is no stranger to the reader. It would not have been difficult for any one to recognise in the lad with the high, white forehead, fine eyes, and dark, close, curling hair the features of young Angus. Ronald, in fact, it was, who, with his left hand on his friend's shoulder, stood watching the rapidly nearing boat with interest and curiosity.

His friend, whose shoulder he so affectionately handled, was a fine stamp of British boyhood. A head and shoulders taller than Ronald, whose senior he was by eighteen months, he was a broad, strapping young fellow, with a bright, clear complexion somewhat tanned by the sun, blue eyes that vied with the turquoise in richness of colouring, and sunny yellow hair with streaks of gold in it, whenever the sun lit up the truant shades, that came and went with every flashing ray. One glance at that boy, and that glance told you that by nature he was born and bred a gentleman. But unlike Ronald, Esca Hamilton had not been born with a golden spoon in his mouth, with wealth and high expectations to look forward to. His father he had never known. A captain in the Royal Artillery, this father had been shot down while working his guns in the Crimean War, and at a moment when victory shone down on the British ranks. His cheery voice, even as death struck him, had rung out a last exhortation to his men, and, as his eyes closed and his head fell back, those men saw the smile of victory lighting up the features of their chief, for whom they would have died a hundred deaths.

Little Esca at this time was only three months old, a bright, plump child, with large blue eyes and soft downy head, whereon the love-locks of later years were already beginning to show themselves. As he crowed and laughed in his mother's arms, and clapped his baby hands, he little knew the sorrow that was bowing down that poor mother's heart, or the great loss she and he had sustained. And Mrs. Hamilton, as she clasped her baby to her heart, and looked down on the only treasure she had left, shuddered as she thought how frail was the thread, that held for her in this world, this one last link of the happy past. On a competency of £270 a year she made her way home to Scotland, and settled down in a tiny cottage left her by her mother, that nestled amidst the wood-clad hills overlooking Loch Moidart.* Here, amidst scenes romantic in the history of Prince Charlie, and lovely to the eye, young Esca Hamilton grew up; leading a wild, free, lonely life, with no one for a companion but his

* Pronounced Moujart.

mother, and here and there a shepherd's or fisherman's son. And for that matter there was no sturdier mountaineer, no more skilful fisherman along the whole sea-coast around, no bolder swimmer or better shot with the gun than Esca. But his idol was the sea, and he would eagerly devour the contents of such books of travel and adventure as con- nected themselves most especially with the great wild waste of water, that he had learnt to know and love so well. His mother superintended his studies, and personally prepared him at his earnest re- quest for the sea. She saw that his heart was set on that profession, and as she had a brother in the Navy who was well in favour at the Admiralty, she felt that

there were opportunities for her darling
in this direction which might not be
forthcoming in any other. Thus it was
that in course of time Esca Hamilton
passed into the *Britannia*, heading the
list of candidates, and proudly carried his
colours out first again on leaving the old
ship for active service. He and Ronald had
first made friends on the training-ship, and
Ronald's delight can well be imagined when,
on quitting it himself two terms later, he
found himself appointed to the *Bucephalus*,
on which his friend was serving.

" How she spins through the water,
Esca!" observed young Angus, as the boat
they had been watching came within two
hundred yards of the ironclad; " I wonder
who that is in the stern?"

" Some one coming to see the Admiral, perhaps," observed Esca, as he shaded his eyes with his left hand and strove to make out the features of the new-comer. " However," he added, " he won't find him at home; you and I will have to entertain him."

" Let's go to the ladder and see what he wants," said Ronald, as he tucked his two hands into his trousers pockets and sauntered slowly forward.

When the two midshipmen reached the spot to which they had directed their foot-steps, they found the boat alongside the ship, and the stranger whom they had previously observed and discussed standing up in the stern.

" Run down, Jenkins," observed Esca to a

sailor standing by, " and see who he is and what he wants."

" Aye, aye, sir," responded the ready tar, scuttling down the ladder at an amazing pace. In a few seconds he returned, and with due formality handed the senior midshipman a gentleman's card.

" That's 'im, sir," he observed, " and he says as 'ow he wants to speak to the Hadmiral if he can ; but if he's hout, then to the hofficer in command."

" Well, as all the officers are ashore but us two, Jenkins, he must speak to me," answered young Hamilton, with just a shade of importance in his tone. " Show him up here."

" Aye, aye, sir," answered that individual promptly.

On receiving the young midshipman's message the stranger leapt lightly on to the landing-stage and came quickly up the ladder. It was easy—as Ronald observed to his friend—to perceive, that the new-comer was "no land lubber."

"You wished to see the Admiral?" inquired Esca courteously. "I am sorry to say he is away on shore. So are all the ship's officers except myself and my friend here; but if you will leave any message with me I will see the Admiral gets it on his return."

"Thank you, sir," answered the stranger, in a low musical voice. He was a tallish man, with very handsome features and dark roving eyes. He sported neither beard, whisker, nor moustache, and this made him appear younger than perhaps he really was.

"The business I had with the Admiral was of a private nature," he continued, in the same low voice. "If you will kindly hand him this card on his return, and say I will call again, I will be very much obliged. Meanwhile, can you tell me whose yacht that is lying at anchor across the bay?"

"That is the *Firefly*, Lord Ettrick's," put in Ronald quickly.

"Oh! thank you, sir," replied the stranger quietly. "You do not by any chance happen to know if a yacht called the *Mayflower* has been here lately or is expected?"

"Yes, I do," answered young Hamilton, "The *Mayflower* was here a week ago, but put out to sea a few hours before the *Firefly* came in, but I don't know her course."

A vicious look came into the roving dark eyes of the stranger. Ronald noticed that he clenched his left hand, and that his lips trembled as if muttering something. He looked disturbed and put about.

" I am obliged, sirs—good-morning," was all he replied, however, as he turned to descend the ladder, at the same time slightly raising his black slouch hat.

The boys returned the salute, and watched his descent and departure curiously. As the boat made for the shore Esca Hamilton examined the card which he held in his hand. It bore no address, merely the name of Mr. Ruys Darrell.

" A queer name," he observed to Ronald, as he slipped the card into his waistcoat pocket. " I wonder who the dickens Mr. Ruys Darrell is ? I took no liking to his face."

" Nor I either," answered young Angus; " he was handsome enough, but there was evil in his eyes, if ever I saw any. I sha'n't forget him easily. But, Esca, there goes eight bells; let's pipe to dinner, I fancy an orange or two and a cool drink. This heat has made me as thirsty as can be."

Down went the two mids to the gun-room, and in the expectation of refreshment the stranger and his evil countenance were for the moment forgotten.

At the same time as this little scene was being enacted, Maeva Doun was seated in

a light ebony rocking-chair on the deck
of her father's beautiful yacht the *Firefly*.
Nearly four months had passed away since
the episodes related in the last chapter had
occurred. When Lady Wrathness in her
hate and vengeance had struck down the
girl that confronted her with a brutal blow
from a knuckle-duster, the child had lain
where the heavy brass instrument had
dropped her, until discovered by her mother
and Ronald. A deep, cruel gash laid open
the clear white forehead, and from the
wound dark streams of blood were flowing,
which made her a terrible sight to behold.
For days this child, the hope and heiress
of the house of Ettrick, lay hovering
between life and death, tenderly and carefully watched by her parents, and the

object of the most anxious solicitude on
all sides. The shock had been most fearful, and the doctors entertained the worst
fears. But the girl's splendid constitution
was proof against everything, and in course
of time she rallied. No sooner had she
been pronounced out of danger than Ronald
returned to the *Britannia*. It being his
final term on that ship, it was necessary
that he should work hard in order to pass
out with honour, which in effect he eventually did.

On one point Maeva remained obsti-
nately silent. She absolutely refused to
give the name of her assailant. Truthfully
she could aver that she knew not where
she dwelt, as in effect she did not. To
have disclosed the name of Lady Wrath-

ness would no doubt have brought about that person's arrest; but this, Maeva argued to herself, would doubtless bode evil to her friend, and bring to light the terrible accusations which his wife had hurled against him in the girl's presence. So the staunch, faithful heart of Maeva remained sealed against all entreaties, and the secret continued locked in her bosom.

Did she believe Lady Wrathness's declaration? Over and over again it reverted to her, and as she repeated the words to herself a terrible shudder would shake the poor child's frame. Ah! how could she believe such evil of him? Surely he was incapable of deeds so foul. And then his last written injunction would well up from the bottom of her heart—that injunction not to believe all the evil that she might hear of him. Was he not far away, a lonely, hunted wanderer, and would she, his great, great friend, doubt him? " Never!" she would exclaim to herself; and then she would sometimes softly add, " And even if I did, I would not forsake him."

Complete change of scene had been expressly enjoined for her by the doctors, and Lord and Lady Ettrick had decided to start on their yachting cruise as quickly as possible. Thus it was that about the middle of January the *Firefly*, 500-ton steam-yacht, and the property of Lord Ettrick, entered Rio Harbour, a few days after the arrival of the Flying Squadron under the command of Admiral Fullerton, whose flag was hoisted on the *Bucephalus*,

whereon young Angus and his friend, Esca
Hamilton, were serving.   The party on
the *Firefly* consisted, in addition to Maeva
and her father and mother, of Sir Alan
Fairfax, a young guardsman, Mr. Herbert,
Lady and Miss Wrottesley, Colonel St.
Leger Slade, and Miss Chambertown. This
latter had been invited at Maeva's earnest
request, and Mrs. Chambertown had gladly
made over her daughter to Lady Ettrick's
care, all the more willingly as Sir Alan
Fairfax was young and rich, and regarded as
the catch of the day ; although so far, he had
not been hooked, in spite of much angling.

Thus it was that Maeva came to be
lying at ease in her ebony rocking-chair on
the snow-white decks of her father's yacht,
beneath the sapphire tropical sky that

looked down on Rio. Every one on board
of the party had betaken themselves on
shore to visit Tijuca, up the mountain
side. But as Maeva had already arranged
to visit that spot on the morrow with
Ronald and young Esca Hamilton, she had
pleaded to be allowed a quiet day on the
yacht, more especially as she and the remainder of the *Firefly* party were engaged
to dine that night on board the *Bucephalus*
with the Admiral.

Why had Rio de Janeiro been chosen
as the first spot to be visited, the reader
may ask? Well, Lord Ettrick had left it
to Maeva to arrange the details of the
voyage. He wished to occupy her mind
and give her as much to think about as
possible, and as soon as the departure had

been settled upon and decided, had in-
formed her to this effect. And Maeva
with glad surprise had joyfully accepted
the situation. In her heart she was longing to make for the South American
coast, and before her father's decision had
been made known to her had made up
her mind to ask him to take that course.
For what reason, it may again be asked?
In Maeva's eyes a very good one, and it
was this.

A few days after her convalescence the
post brought her amongst several other
letters a thick one in a strange handwriting. Instinctively Maeva felt it concerned her absent friend. Why, she knew
not, and could not have told any one, but
still the feeling was there, and she accord-

ingly slipped the letter unopened into her
pocket. When later on in the quiet of her
own room she got an opportunity to read
it, the girl's resolve was taken. She must
get to America somehow. She must en-
deavour to fathom and solve what to her
appeared a terrible tale. By God's help
she must unravel the truth and save her
friend from the meshes which his enemies
were casting around him. Maeva knew
that the task before her was overwhelm-
ing. But her heart was brave, her
courage true, and she felt that no hope
remained for her in life unless she could
succeed. As her purpose may appear
strange to those who are ignorant of
what prompted it, the next chapter will
introduce this letter to the reader.

CHAPTER XII.

"GIRL," it began, "if in my path of vengeance you choose to throw yourself, upon your own head be the fatal results. Why do I write this, but to satisfy in part my vengeance on him who has dared to love you and hate me? And because I hate him in return, hate him more than the English language can express, I have told you that, which I know he would have given his life, that you should not know. Well, I have paid him out so far; read on, girl, and learn who and what your paramour is.

"You are too young to remember Harold

Darrell when he was a young man of twenty-three. He is twelve years older now, and is my Lord Wrathness. Would you like to know how he came by that title, and made me my Lady Wrathness twice over? Have I not told you that it was by murder? Read on, and you shall know.

"It was but twelve years ago that I was a young and beautiful girl. Not so young as you, for you are a mere child; but I was a girl, still in my teens, and accounted lovely. I was a native of New Brunswick; what my name was matters not to you, nor need be told for the purpose of my story. I dwelt in Newcastle on the Miramichi River, an orphan, for I had lost both father and mother; and my guardians and trustees were two lawyers, whom we will call Mr. F. and Mr. C. There came to Newcastle on or about the time I am relating two young Britishers from across the Atlantic. One was a white-faced, frail, and sickly youth; the other, a handsome, good-looking young man. The former was Ruthven, Earl of Wrathness; the latter, Harold Darrell, his cousin. They brought letters of introduction to my guardians, who received them with much cordiality and *empressement*.

" Long did these two tarry at Newcastle. They used to make lengthy expeditions up country together on shooting or fishing ventures; but they always returned to the busy town on the Miramichi River, where I and my guardians dwelt. It was not

difficult to learn the attraction which, with
magnetic influence appeared to bring them
back again and again to the same spot.
That attraction was myself. Both Ruthven
and Darrell loved me.

" And I, was my heart fancy free ? It
was not. I too had given it away, but in
the eyes of my guardians to the wrong
man. I had given it to Darrell.

" Full well I knew that I had erred,
but like Messrs. F. and C. I coveted a
Countess's coronet. I determined, therefore,
to marry the pale-faced youth, though I
loved his handsome cousin ; but then the
former was rich, and had great estates—
the latter was burdened with nought but
a poor man's portion. The inevitable soon
arrived. Both men proposed, I accepted

the puny earl whom I loathed, rejected the penniless but handsome Harold Darrell, whom I loved. I shall never forget his face, half angry, half despairing, when I told him I was to be his cousin's wife. But so it was, and in due course of time I became Countess of Wrathness. Harold Darrell did not attend our wedding. He went about moody and oppressed. He appeared to be rapt in deep thought, to be continually in dreamland.

" Suddenly, however, he seemed to become reconciled to his fate and comforted. He grew cordial and friendly with his cousin. They were frequently together once more, and apparently fast friends. North-west of Newcastle, by the Big Hole, is situated 'the Indian Reserve.'

Now near this Big Hole is a curious cave, called by the Micmac Indians 'Condean Weegan,' or 'the stone wigwam.' Thither Harold Darrell invited his cousin to accompany him one lovely afternoon, and with another man they started in a small boat, ostensibly to visit the cave. Girl, from this expedition the Earl never returned. His cousin came back, pale and saturated, with a trumped-up story of how the former had slipped from the cave's ledge into the water, and sunk before aid could reach him. His tale was corroborated by the man who had accompanied him, but who soon after mysteriously disappeared. This man, however, is not dead, and he has since described to me the foul murder committed by Harold Darrell, now Lord Wrathness, my second husband, a murderer, and your lover. He has told me how the wretch took his opportunity when his cousin was standing unawares to push him from the ledge, and then retire out of sight into the cave, leaving his helpless relative, who could not swim, to drown. The only eye-witness of this foul deed was my informant. His mouth was closed by a promise of a large annual annuity, and he dwells now in affluence and ease at Rio Janeiro. But nevertheless he is my man, and a word from me will open his lips to denounce the murderer, whenever and however it shall please me to dictate to him. Girl, your lover's fate is in my hands; I, his lawful wife, whom he has scorned and now jilts for you.

" How did I become his wife, you ask ? The murder foul still stained his hands when he renewed his suit, and I, *then* knowing nothing, accepted him, married the man I loved, and for a second time became Lady Wrathness. There is no necessity for me to relate more, to tell you why and how in time my love turned to hate. I have told you enough to accomplish the first act of my vengeance. I can now proceed to my second. Nay, do not seek to dare me, or warn him. Interference on your part will but hasten his doom. He has fled from my vengeance, but all in vain ; I will track him and follow him to the uttermost ends of the earth, till I have brought his proud, haughty spirit to bay ; and then I will denounce him, and bring him to the gallows for the hideous crime of murder."

Pale to the lips and with a beating heart Maeva had read that letter, not once, not twice, but over and over again. The trial was a terrible one, but the girl was brave, and true as steel. Appearances were strongly in favour of the charge. If Wrathness was not guilty, why had he fled in this sudden, mysterious manner, without leaving a clue to his whereabouts? If he had nothing to fear why shun publicity? All these and many such questions would rise unbidden to her lips ; yet above them all she seemed to read in letters of fire his imploring entreaty that she would not believe all the ill she heard of him.

"O God! Harold," she would whisper softly to herself, " I love you, and I will not forsake you. What is life to me if I cannot help you and clear you from this terrible charge? It may be some foul plot of which you are the victim. If so, I will find it out ; I will trace it and lay it bare. Harold, dear Harold, I will redeem your fair name, aye, even if it be in my own blood."

And alone with her terrible secret, Maeva, to whom it was ever present, had determined, by hook or by crook, to trace in Rio Janeiro the man referred to by Lady Wrathness as the witness of that awful, ghastly deed.

She had arrived, as we have seen, at her destination, and it was agreed that a three weeks' or a month's stay should be made at Rio. There was plenty to be seen, and long expeditions up country planned in all directions by different members of the party. Lord and Lady Ettrick had been invited by an old friend and settler in those parts to visit him in his orange ranch far away up in the blue Oregon Mountains, which loomed high against the deep-tinted sky at the head of the harbour; and as Maeva begged to be allowed to remain on the yacht, on the plea of seeing as much as possible of Ronald, her mother had decided on taking Miss Chambertown with her, and Sir Alan Fairfax had been also invited to accompany them.

And so it was that on the day in question Maeva sat silent and thoughtful on the deck of the *Firefly*, gazing at the blue sky above and revolving future plans in her mind.

It should be related that during the week the *Firefly* had been in harbour Ronald had been a frequent visitor on board, and on several occasions had been accompanied by Esca Hamilton. With this latter, Maeva had struck up a great friendship. The boy's bright, open, handsome countenance had attracted her instinctively, and he,—well, if the truth must be said, let it be acknowledged that young Esca had fallen hopelessly over head and ears in love with his friend's cousin.

" Lady Maeva isn't a bit like any other girl I've ever seen, Ronald," he had said; "there is only one person she reminds me of, and that is my own dear mother ;" and

Ronald, who was always ready to sympathise with any one who admired his dearly-loved cousin, had nodded his head and replied confidentially, " Wait, my boy, till you know her a bit better, and then you will agree with me that there's no one in the world that can ever come up to Maeva."

That evening the two friends stood side by side where they had stood that morning, this time watching for the arrival of the *Firefly* party. Ronald had been invited to dine with the Admiral, and was therefore arrayed in full evening dress, and Esca, who had just come off duty, had joined him by the taffrail. Close to the landing-stage a small boat bobbed up and down, with a single oarsman therein, who resting on his oars was apparently waiting for some one.   That some one was closeted with the Admiral.

" Hark, Ronald ! that's them," exclaimed Esca suddenly.   The young midshipman had been leaning on his arms looking over the ship's side, and listening intently.   As he spoke the measured rapid stroke of several well-handled oars came sounding along the water, and making for the *Bucephalus*   Fortunately dusk had set in, or the tell-tale flush that dyed young Hamilton's face, throat, and neck would have unfolded the secret of his heart.   As it was, he alone knew it.

Quickly the boat glided alongside the great ship, and the two midshipmen were at its head in a moment, helping the whole party to disembark.   As they ascended the ladder steps Esca managed to get beside Maeva, and was conversing gaily with her, when on reaching the deck they perceived the Admiral approaching to greet his visitors. Close behind him followed the tall, slight form of a man wearing a loose cloak and black slouch hat. As Admiral Fullerton shook hands with Lord and Lady Ettrick, and was introduced to those of the party who were strangers to him, the cloaked figure passed them silently, and glided quietly by Esca and Maeva, who were standing just in the glare of a swinging lantern. As he did so, its light fell full upon his face, disclosing his features plainly and distinctly. Maeva, who had been watching him, suddenly uttered a low cry and grasped Esca's arm.

"Tell me," she exclaimed, in a hurried breathless voice, "tell me, Mr. Hamilton, who is that man?"

"Why, I declare it's the same fellow who was here this morning, wanting to see Admiral Fullerton," answered the youth, in a surprised tone. "I don't know who he is. Stay!" he added suddenly, "I do though, in a way, because he left his card with me, and Mr. Ruys Darrell was printed on it; but who Ruys Darrell is I do not know."

The party were beginning to move towards the Admiral's cabin. Maeva took a desperate resolution.

"Mr. Hamilton," she said hurriedly, "I believe we are good friends—will you do me a favour?"

" Anything in the wide world," answered the boy, his heart bounding with loyalty and delight.

" Then follow that man, find out for me where he lives, and let me know as soon as ever you can. Oh ! if you knew all that depends on my learning it, you would do it. I cannot explain,—see, they are all going in,—will you ? "

There was an agonised sound in her voice, a world of entreaty. Her great grey eyes looked him full in the face. What mattered all the world to young Esca ? Had she not asked him to do something ? He would have died rather than refuse.

" Trust me," was all he answered ; but there was a ring in his voice which told her that *she could trust him.*

"Maeva dear, come on!" called out Lord Ettrick; and the girl had to hurry forward, leaving Esca standing alone.

The lad looked down at the bobbing boat below him,—the stranger was preparing to enter it. Then he looked up at the darkling sky above him, and pushed the yellow curls that gathered on his forehead from off it. Then he pulled out his watch, and consulted its face by the light of the lantern. "I have two good hours," he muttered to himself. "I sha'n't be missed, I can do it in that time." He glided along the deck into darkness, and made for the ship's stern. A second later and he had concealed his boots and watch behind a big coil of rope. Then he made fast a thinner rope to an iron stanchion, threw, it over the side of the ship, nimbly followed it, and before the boat was pushed off had let himself silently down and dropped into the water. The next moment he was swimming with strong powerful strokes in the direction of Rio.

He had about a quarter of a mile of water to get through. The distance was nothing to the strong, athletic boy. He could swim almost before he could toddle, and the water was second nature to him. It was blowing, and the water was a bit disturbed, but he had not battled with the wild waves and angry surf of Scotland's western coasts in vain, and the experience and knowledge he had gained therein stood him now in good stead. But Esca had two fears troubling him as he moved rapidly along. One was that the boat containing the stranger would reach Rio before him ; the other was that sharks might do for him between the ship and the shore. It was not for himself that he feared. Esca was not thinking of that. His one thought was to carry out Maeva's wish. His one longing, to be able to show himself worthy of her trust.

Brave, gallant young Esca! Ah, little Maeva knew, as she sat at the Admiral's cosy dinner-table, in what a manner the chivalrous lad was carrying out her behest! He was racing through the water now, and the lights of Rio loomed larger and brighter every minute. He could hear the muffled sound of the boat's oars not far behind him, and he knew that it was gaining upon him. Every inch of strength in him was strained to make headway. Never in his life before had he exerted the great physical powers with which he was gifted to such an extraordinary extent. He deserved to win, did this heroic boy ; and he did. With a heart beating with joy he heard the boat cease rowing, and a movement of feet in her sounded to him o'er the water. It gave him the assurance that the oarsman was attending to something in the craft itself. It encouraged him to renewed exertion.

Suddenly the sound of surf struck his ear. He could have shouted for joy. It told him that land lay close ahead. He threw himself on his back and took a long wind, preparatory to breasting the breakers.

Then he struck out once more. In another second he was in the surf and fighting his way through it as it tossed him to and fro. He heard its sullen roar breaking on the beach ; he fought his way inch by inch, sinking ever and anon to feel if he could touch ground. Something struck his foot ; two more powerful strokes and he was within his depth. In another moment he was on dry land, and racing with all his might towards the landing-pier. Just in time, too, to catch sight of the boat gliding to the landing-stage, and to re-cognise it as the stranger's craft. The young midshipman drew back into the darkness and kept his eyes fixed on the man. He could watch him easily from the spot where he stood concealed. He saw him pay the oarsman off, and then walk away at a rapid swinging pace. Springing down to where the boat lay, the boy made its owner understand in a few disjointed words that it would be required in half an hour ; then away he made after the vanishing figure, and dogged him with footsteps all the more silent inasmuch as he was bootless. Suddenly the stranger paused at a corner street door and knocked with his stick. It was quickly opened, the object of pursuit entered, and the door closed upon him.

" Thank God !" was all that Esca exclaimed as he took note of the house, street, and locality. " I have accomplished what *she* asked me."

He said no more, but hurried back to

where the boat lay waiting for him. As he did so he felt in his trousers pockets and his face brightened.

" I've enough here to pay the fellow," he soliloquised ; " how glad I am I did not spend it all ! "

He sat silently in the boat till the great black hull of the *Bucephalus* hove in sight. Then he stood up, signed to the man rowing to rest on his oars, and handing him several silver pieces pointed to the ship, and signified his intention of swimming to it, at the same time placing his first finger on his lips in a warning attitude. The man winked and smiled. Evidently Esca had overpaid him.

" Young gentleman out on lark. Me no peach, me only watch see you get up safe." He had not finished his remarks when Esca was overboard and swimming for the ship. The man sat still in his boat, with a broad grin on his face. He saw Esca reach the ironclad, seize the rope, and pull himself hand over hand up the side and disappear over the top. Then he dipped his oars in the water and pulled once more for land.

Half an hour later the Admiral stood taking leave of his guests. As he did so Esca in a dry suit sauntered up to where Maeva was standing.

"It is all right, Lady Maeva," he whispered; "I've made out where the person lives, and I'll point you out the house when we go on shore to-morrow."

"Thank God!" he heard her mutter to

herself; and then she added, " How can I thank you, Mr Hamilton?"

He wanted no thanks. He was amply rewarded by the earnest, grateful look in her grave, sad grey eyes. He held out his hand with a boyish impulse.

" I don't want to be thanked, I would do anything *for you.* I would swim until I drowned to serve you." The water was still glistening on his yellow hair; she started as she noticed it.

" Gracious!" she exclaimed, " how did you get to Rio?"

" I swam there," he answered quietly.

" Swam?" She said no more; Admiral Fullerton was facing her, and offering her his hand. Mechanically she held out her own and uttered a courteous good-night, but once more the great, grey eyes strayed to where Esca stood, and if ever eyes spoke those did at that moment. The boy read in them the word, "gratitude."

He slept that night soundly, did that young officer, though his sleep was visited by dreams. And in that sleep he smiled, and his lips moved. They uttered but two words, and these were, "Mother"—"Maeva."

CHAPTER XIII.

THE party on the *Firefly* had broken up for the time being. Lord and Lady Ettrick, Miss Chambertown, and Sir Alan Fairfax had gone to the Oregon Mountains. Mr. Herbert and Colonel St. Leger Slade had started on an inland expedition; and Lady and Miss Wrottesley and Maeva were all that remained on the yacht. Of these last three named, the two former had relations living just outside Rio, and were therefore a good deal absent, which gave Maeva all her time to herself. She had landed in the yellow, unhealthy-looking town with Ronald and

Esca the day following upon the events related in the latter end of the last chapter, and while her cousin had gone in search of a carriage and four mules which was to convey them up to Tijuca, Maeva and Esca had walked through the market-place and turned up a side street leading therefrom. On reaching the far end Esca had pointed out a tall, narrow, four-storied house, at the same time remarking, " It was there, Lady Maeva, that Mr. Ruys Darrell entered last night."

" Thank you, Mr. Hamilton," Maeva had replied ; and then she added quickly, " It must seem very funny to you that I should ask you to track a totally unknown person in the way I did. The story is one that will need explanation, and I think it is only fair that in so far as it is possible I should tell it to you. You are my friend, are you not? Yet why should I ask you? No one but a true, good friend would have done what you did for me last night, and I shall never forget it No, never."

"If I rendered you ever so slight a service, Lady Maeva," had answered the boy, "I only ask for one reward, and that is that you will trust me. I am not exactly like most boys. My only public school training has been the *Britannia*. Till then I was always with my dear, dear mother. She used to talk to me about everything, and we were all in all to each other. I think I could understand and sympathise with you in any trouble or bother you liked to confide in me. Of course I know I am only a boy, not quite seventeen yet ; but I am old enough to feel what friendship means, and as you say you believe I am your friend, let me— please let me—do all I can to help you and to show it."

"And I am only a girl," had answered Maeva simply ; "but I see no reason why a boy and girl should not be as firm friends as any one else. Ronald and I have been firm friends since baby days, and yet somehow or other, love him as I do, I could not tell him what I mean to tell you the first opportunity I can get to speak with you alone."

And the boy's fair face had flushed with a rosy glow of new-found happiness. Everything looked beautiful in his eyes; even the dirty streets of Rio became lovely.

They had got back to the market-place, and even as they arrived there the clank of trotting feet and rumbling wheels struck upon their ears. In a few minutes Ronald hove in sight, sitting in state in the very centre of the back seat of a vehicle which might be happily described as something between a landau and victoria. Drawing it were four smart, somewhat restive-looking mules, who were coming along at a famous pace, under the Jehuship of a sallow-looking Portuguese individual.

No sooner did Ronald perceive his friends than he stood up in the carriage and began waving his cap round his head, much to the amusement of several passers-by, who stood and stared at the demonstrative young Britisher; while Esca, who was brimming over with happiness and excitement, waved back a glad response. The mule carriage drew up immediately it came in sight of the market-place, and stood awaiting the arrival of the midshipman and Maeva. Just as the two were about to step into it, however, and Ronald was volubly talking, a marine stepped up, and, saluting this latter, handed him a note.

"What can it be?" exclaimed the young earl, as he opened it curiously; but the next moment his face fell. "All right, Brett," he said quietly; "say I'll

be on board immediately;" then, as the
marine saluted and marched off, Ronald
turned ruefully to Esca and Maeva.

"It's no go," he remarked, in a disappointed tone; "the Admiral wants me;
therefore, so far as I am concerned, our
jolly expedition to Tijuca is at an end.
Never mind though," he added, as he saw
his cousin about to speak, "you go,
Maeva, with Esca; I've seen the place
before, so it does not matter. If I can
get away later on I'll follow you up.
I know where I can hire a horse, and
then I can easily catch you. So good-
bye, Esca, old man; do you and Maeva
take good care of each other, and if I
can I'll soon be with you."

Saying which, poor Ronald, who was

frightfully disappointed, but who put a brave face on the matter, walked off briskly towards the landing-stage.

Left standing by themselves, Esca and Maeva looked at one another.

" Shall we go?" he inquired, doubtfully.

"Oh yes," answered Maeva, quickly; " Ronald is sure to get away soon, and then I know he will be quickly with us; meanwhile we can drive up in this conveyance, and when we get to Tijuca I can tell you what I said I would."

She signed him to get in as she spoke, and Esca was quickly by her side. The driver was bidden to drive to Tijuca. He started at a gallop, and the boy and girl were soon on the outskirts of Rio, driving along between cool-looking villas, half hidden in a wealth of tropical flowers and vegetation.

Soon the region of houses became scarcer; they had begun to mount upwards, the road leading through tropical forest, in and out of which gorgeous butterflies and bright - plumaged birds winged their flight and fluttered. Giant ferns made the roadway bright with their graceful foliage; the busy hum was ever in the air, and above all this wealth of beauty and glory the sapphire sky looked down in its mantle of deep dark blue.

"How gloriously beautiful!" exclaimed Maeva, as a bend in the road and a rift in the forest disclosed far away below the great sheening land-locked bay of

Rio Harbour; " I don't think I ever saw anything more beautiful in my life. Oh! why does not every one travel and see the world?"

" There are plenty who would like to," laughed Esca Hamilton, " if they could only get the chance;" and then he added, a shade more seriously, " I know one who has often yearned to do so, and that was my dear mother."

" Then why hasn't she ? " inquired Maeva, in an interested voice; but she felt sorry after, that she had asked the question.

" Because neither I nor mother are like you and Ronald, Lady Maeva," answered Esca, with just a shade of bitterness in his voice. " We were not born with

golden spoons in our mouths. It is easy
enough for people like you and Ronald
to gratify every whim and taste, when
money is not wanting. But it is different
for poor paupers like myself, who haven't
a mag of their own, and who must
depend on themselves for their livelihood.
Not that I should complain, though.
Were it not for the best and most
unselfish of mothers I should not be
following the profession that I love. God
bless her! Think of all she must have
sacrificed for me, to be able to put me
in the navy and give me an allowance out
of £270 a year. Dear, kind old mother!"

"Oh! how glad I am to hear you
speak of your mother like that, Mr.
Hamilton," exclaimed Maeva warmly.

"There is nothing like one's mother. Mine is one of the very best, too, and I owe everything in the world to her. But don't mind being poor, will you? I am sure you will get on in your profession and do well; and think how happy Mrs. Hamilton will be if you do."

"Would it please you also?" asked Esca, and there was a pleading ring in his boyish voice as he asked the question.

"Please me? I should just think it would! I shall always be interested in what you do. Are you not my friend? It is but natural that I should," replied the girl simply, as she looked into his blue pleading eyes with her large, grave, grey ones.

And so they talked away, as the carriage

with its foam-flecked mules mounted higher
and higher through the tropical forest of
Tijuca.   Esca Hamilton's boyish heart
was in a flame; the moments flew all too
quickly by; he found himself longing that
they could last for ever, wondering what
he had ever done to merit so much
happiness.   And let those who may be
inclined to smile at this early evidence
of a boy's love, and incredulously doubt
its existence, bear in mind that there is
probably no purer, no nobler, no more
unselfish devotion than that which finds
its birth in a boy's first love.   It is un-
doubtedly the truest passion of a man's
lifetime.

They reached the summit of the forest-
crowned mountain at length, and turning

sharply to the right, after descending a
short but steep incline, were whisked up
to the doors of Tijuca. A long, white,
two-storied, verandahed house, looking
cool and inviting to the dusty traveller,
stood facing them, and they were soon
seated in the shade, enjoying a cool ice
and some delicious fruit which the hos-
pitable proprietor, an old friend of Lord
Ettrick's, insisted on at once placing
before them.

Then, when they had finished, the boy
and girl strolled away into the forest, and
amidst its wealth of loveliness, beside a
dark, clear pool of water, the two sat down
side by side, while Maeva unfolded to her
boy-friend the terrible secret of which she
was possessed. She told him all but one

thing. She told him of her childhood's days with Ronald, of his noble home and hers; and how at length had come amongst them the young earl with the dark, sad eyes, who had risked his life to gratify her whim, whom she in turn had rescued. She told the young midshipman of the friendship that had grown up between them, of the earl's sudden disappearance, of his letters, and lastly of the visit of Lady Wrathness and its cruel result; and then she took from her pocket that bad woman's letter, and, with an omission here and there, read it to him almost in its entirety. But one thing she did not tell Esca. She did not tell him of the love that lay next her heart. That was a secret which she could breathe to no one, which she herself was the sole confidant of. She spoke of Wrathness as a friend, as one whom she must save for friendship's sake, and nothing more.

But love's sight is keen. It sees what other eyes are blind to, and the boy instinctively guessed the truth. For the first time in his life a feeling shot through the openhearted, generous spirit of young Esca, —a feeling that made him for the moment almost hate the man who, in his eyes, appeared to have unlawfully stolen the love and allegiance of the girl before him. It was a feeling that can never be acutely felt in all its intensity save in conjunction with love. Esca was jealous. The fact that she was not fancy free, though yet so young a child, broke in upon his happy, exulting heart with a bleak, bitter reality. He could hardly stand the revelation, it had been so sudden and so unexpected. He rose up from where he had been sitting and walked moodily into the forest, leaving her by the dark, glassy pool alone. A terrible battle was going on within him,—it was the struggle of Love and Jealousy. Boy though he was, it raged there in all its fiercest intensity; it burned into his very soul.

"O God!" he exclaimed passionately, a few minutes ago I was so happy, and now—now——" He broke off abruptly and stamped his foot; the nobler side of his character was gaining the mastery.

"Selfish brute that I am!" he muttered.

" I love her,—aye, ever so dearly, and this
is how I show it, moaning over myself
while she is left to her sad thoughts and
terrible trouble. Oh! mother, this is not
the unselfish lesson which your brave,
sweet example has ever taught your boy
to love, look up to, and respect. But I
will be brave, I will be her friend, I will
help her by God's good help! If I can
only make her happy what more can I
want or expect? and perhaps—perhaps some
day she will know how I loved her."

He uttered the last words very softly;
a gleam shone in his blue eyes, and he
tossed the yellow love-locks from his high
white forehead as he turned and went
back to where she was sitting. She looked
up at him half fearfully. No idea of what

his thoughts had been, of the struggle he
had been going through, appeared to strike
her. She dreaded that she had done wrong
in telling him what she had, and that
appearances against Lord Wrathness were
too strong for the boy to be able to look at
matters in the same light as she did. This
was why, no doubt, he had walked away
and left her sitting alone. But Maeva,
attracted to Esca as she had been, did not
know yet all the nobility of the boy's nature.

He came and sat down once more beside
her, and this time took her hand in his.
How his own trembled as he did so! and
his face was very white.

"Thank you, Lady Maeva," he said
very gently, "for confiding your trouble to
me. God grant that I may be able to

be of use to you. Trust me to do any mortal thing I can, and that I will, though I am only a poor boy midshipman. Never while you live, though you may have many a better, will you have a truer or more devoted friend than Esca Hamilton."

" Thank you, thank you, Esca—I mean Mr. Hamilton," she exclaimed warmly.

" Oh, call me Esca—do please call me that," he burst out quickly ; " I cannot tell you how happy it would make me."

" Then I will do so," she answered simply ; "but only on condition that you call me Maeva."

" But what would Lord and Lady Ettrick say to that ? " he inquired doubtfully ; " wouldn't they think it awfully cheeky ? "

" Not they," she answered with a slight

laugh; "why, what harm is there in a girl and boy friend calling each other by their Christian names? Shall it be agreed?"

"Agreed," he replied.

"And now," she continued, "you must let me tell you something more, Esca. Do you know why I was so startled when I saw that man pass us on the *Bucephalus*, and why I begged you to find out for me where he lived? Who do you think he was? I could not be mistaken,—no, that would be impossible. Esca, that Mr. Ruys Darrell is no man. That stranger was Lady Wrathness."

He started. "The devil he was!" he exclaimed; and then added quickly, "I beg your pardon."

"And she means mischief," continued

Maeva excitedly, not noticing the interruption; " I feel sure she is tracking Lord Wrathness."

" I remember now," put in Esca, " that yesterday morning, when this stranger first boarded the *Bucephalus* and asked for Admiral Fullerton, he put questions to me as to whom the *Firefly* belonged to, and then inquired if the *Mayflower* had been here or was expected. I replied that the latter yacht had been in harbour, and only left a few hours before the arrival of the *Firefly*."

" What! the *Mayflower* has been here ? " burst from Maeva's lips, while a bright crimson flush dyed her cheeks. Esca heard her voice quiver and saw the red blood mount. He shuddered.

"Yes, Maeva." He said the name very tenderly, but she hardly heard him; she was staring in front of her with a startled, troubled expression.

"Maeva," said young Esca,—he spoke in a quiet firm voice,—"listen to me. I see it all quite plainly now. Lord Wrathness has been here probably to see the man who is pensioned here, and Lady Wrathness is here, no doubt, for the same reason. We must go back to Rio, and I will find out for you the name of the man. I have very little doubt that he lives in the same house as that into which the stranger, whom you declare to be Lady Wrathness, entered last night. Let me do this for you, and meanwhile I will have a real good think over the whole matter, and do

the best I can to advise you and help
you. Cheer up, we will work together,
and by God's help we will unravel the
plot, for a plot I feel sure it is. I feel
certain that your friend is innocent, although
appearances are dead against him."

" Oh ! thank you, thank you, dear Esca ;
how can I ever repay such a true, good
friend as you ?" exclaimed Maeva, the great
tears welling up into her eyes. She had
borne this secret trouble by herself so long,
that it was like a heaven-sent ray in a
dark night, to feel that she had some one
with whom to share it, and to whom she
could open her heart.

He bent down and kissed the little hand
that he held in his, tenderly, passionately.
" I don't want to be repaid," he said

gently, "all I want is to help you. All
I want is that you will let me serve you,
work for you, die for you, be to you a
true friend."

She did not answer. Her heart was
too full for words. Yet, grateful as Maeva
felt, deeply as she appreciated the boy's
genuine, practical friendship, she had not
read the secret that lay next his heart.

*   *   *   *   *

That same night a tall handsome young
midshipman stood outside the door of that
corner house into which the stranger had
disappeared the day before. He had just
rung the bell. A negro slave opened it.

" Can I see the master ? " asked the
young officer in broken Portuguese.

The negro smiled. " Me talkee Een--glish," he said.

" Well, can I see your master ? " said the midshipman, impatiently, this time in English.

The negro motioned him to enter, and led the way along a cool, flower-scented corridor, which led into an open and verandahed courtyard. Waving his hand in the direction of a tiny fountain that was playing in the centre, and which was lighted up with fancy lanterns, the negro grinned, and having remarked, " There be massa," turned and disappeared.

The midshipman looked in front of him, and perceived seated near the fountain an apparently elderly man, in whose hair grey threads were gathering quickly. He was reading.

. "Ahem!" coughed the youthful officer.

The elderly man started and looked up. On perceiving the midshipman he rose quickly.

"To whom am I indebted for the honour of a visit?" he inquired courteously, in a somewhat American accent.

"I must excuse myself," answered Esca —for the midshipman was no other—in an apologetic tone, "but I came to ask if Mr. Ruys Darrell, who called on Admiral Fullerton yesterday, is staying here."

"He was," answered the elderly man, eyeing his visitor keenly; "that is to say, he arrived here yesterday by the Pacific Steam Navigation Company's liner the *Valparaiso*, which left for Chili this afternoon, and Mr. Ruys Darrell went on in her."

" Can you give me his address for the Admiral?" asked Esca, perhaps a shade too eagerly.

" I am sorry I cannot oblige you," answered the elderly man, " but if any information is required, or if there is anything that I can do for Admiral Fullerton in the place of Mr. Darrell, pray mention that I shall be charmed."

" Thank you, I will ask him ; may I ask your name ?" here put in Esca.

" Certainly," replied the personage addressed ; " my name is Richard Emerson."

" Thank you, sir," said Esca, as he prepared to withdraw. " I hope you will excuse me for this late intrusion."

" Do not mention it," answered the elderly man, who had a haggard, worn appearance, as he touched a little bell standing on a table close beside him. The negro slave appeared.

" Show this gentleman out, Tim," he said.

" Good-night, sir," observed Esca, as he turned to follow the slave.

" Good-night, sir," responded the elderly man ; and Esca noticed that there was a weary ring in his voice.

CHAPTER XIV.

"AND if I tell you, Lady Maeva Doun, am I to clearly understand that the price of this information is to be £10,000 and your solemn and most sacred word that the informant will not be disclosed?"

"You have my solemn word of honour."

Such was the question and reply put by Richard Emerson, introduced to the reader in the last chapter, and Maeva Doun. They were standing in the same verandahed courtyard where Esca had intruded on the former occasion, when he had discovered the gentleman in question. Maeva was standing leaning against the fountain, her two hands clasped together, and he with the rapidly-silvering hair, careworn expression, and weary voice was pacing up and down, his hands behind him, his head bent low, his step hurried and slouching. As he put this question, however, he stood still and faced her, and she, with her great grey eyes fixed steadily upon him, with he bright, honest expression of one who could not lie, had answered him in the words above quoted.

There came a gleam into his sunken eyes, a nervous twitching about his thin pale lips. His hands unclasped themselves, and appeared to be clutching at something which he seemed to see in front of him, and as he stood thus the girl heard him mutter the words, "Gold, I shall have more gold."

She looked at him with a feeling of repulsion as she said, "You have my word of honour, Mr. Emerson, on condition that you tell me the full truth and hide nothing from me. Provided you do this, the money is yours, and your individuality as informant safe in my hands. I would die sooner than betray you."

"I believe you," he said, in a low voice; "intimate as I am and have been with sin, and crime, and wickedness, I know, nevertheless, what a great and noble nature is, for I had once a mother. Ah! Lady Maeva, bad as I am, I was not always what you see me now, till temptation beset, overcame me, and led me astray."

He paused and covered his eyes with both hands, and his silvering head bowed down upon them. Suddenly he raised it up, and looked once more at the girl.

"Ask me what questions you will," he said, and began pacing up and down the court again.

She leant more heavily against the fountain pillar, and her hands clasped tighter together.

"Were you a witness to Lord Wrathness's murder, and was the murderer Harold Darrell?" she inquired abruptly. He stopped in his hurried pacing, and looked straight at her. His answer came slowly, but distinctly.

"Yes, Lady Maeva, I was a witness of that murder, yet, though Harold Darrell was present, he did not do the deed. Nevertheless, he who is now Lord Wrathness believes that he did do it."

Maeva sprang forward and seized the man's hands. There was a happy smile on her lips. " You swear that, and can prove it, can you ? " she cried eagerly ; and as he nodded his head she added, " Is the murderer alive ? "

" He is."

" Oh, thank God! thank God!" she exclaimed fervently. " Harold, dear Harold, I felt, I knew you were innocent. Ah! if I ever doubted you for a moment you will forgive me, for your dear fair name shall be redeemed."

She hardly knew what she was saying, her brain seemed on fire with joy. The terrible burden of doubt and uncertainty which had clung there for so long seemed to have vanished into thin air. Suddenly, however, she turned once more to her informant.

" And the murderer, who is he ? where is he ? " she inquired.

" I am he ! "

He stood facing her, standing so close to her as he hissed out his reply that she started back in horror and dread.

" You ? " she cried.

" Yes, I."

She retreated back to her old place by the fountain, still eyeing him with horror. For a minute or two both kept silence. He was the first to break it.

" If you will sit down on that chair,

Lady Maeva," he said, "you shall hear my story. What I have to tell you will not take very long. It will tell you all you need to know, and will clear Lord Wrathness's name. But remember every word I utter is for you alone. Bear in mind what you have promised."

She made a gesture of assent—she could not bring herself to speak. Mechanically she took the chair he pointed out to her and sat down, her eyes riveted on his face.

He could not bear the look in those great grey eyes, so he sat down beside a writing-table and half covered his face with one hand, against which he leant it. Then in a low distinct voice he began his story :—

" I was twelve years ago," he said, " a native of New Brunswick, and dwelt in Chatham, on the south bank of the Miramichi river, about twenty miles from its mouth. My mother was a Scotch woman; my father, who had died when I was a child, a native of New York. Twelve years ago I was employed as head clerk in the saw mills belonging to Messrs. Cunard and Co., on the river just named, and I was thirty years of age.

" In my capacity as head clerk I had a good deal of what we called *moving work* in those days. This meant *travelling* about to neighbouring towns and transacting business with different firms and lawyers. One saw a certain amount of life in this manner, and made a fair number of acquaintances.

" Well, in the course of my business travels I became acquainted with a certain pair of sharp lawyers called Messrs. Fleecem and Catchem, who were reckoned smart fellows in those parts. There were dark stories afloat of how they had made their money and established themselves as a firm ; but people were not too particular as to their antecedents, and reckoned more their ability and business capacity than anything else.

" Messrs. Fleecem and Catchem dwelt in Newcastle, which stands on the opposite side of the river to Chatham, and with them dwelt an orphan girl named Madeline Dartrey. No one knew who

she was nor whence she came, and
though Messrs. Fleecem and Catchem
called her their ward, people shook their
heads and did not take kindly to the
story. But whoever she was, she possessed
that which no one could dispute, and
that was beauty. I never shall forget
her as I first saw her. She was nine-
teen years of age, and from the moment
I set eyes upon her I fell madly over
head and ears in love with her.

"Madeline Dartrey did not repulse me
altogether, but she would not accept the
proposal of marriage which I made to
her. She took my presents, made good
use of me—I fetched and carried for
her like a dog; but she told me that
unless I could bring her wealth with my

hand she would not marry me. Such a response to so much abject devotion should have opened my eyes to her true character, but I was too madly, too blindly in love, and saw nothing, thought of nothing but how to gain her affections and win her as my wife.

" About this time there suddenly appeared in the locality two young Englishmen, who had arrived in that part of the world presumably to hunt and fish. They applied to Messrs. Fleecem and Catchem for information respecting the best places to enjoy those amusements, and at the latter's cordial invitation arranged to make the lawyers' abode their head-quarters. Until they came, Lady Maeva, my life had been an honest one.

I had spent the greater part of it with my aged mother, whose only hope and support I was. She had ever striven to bring me up honourably and righteously to do my duty, speak the truth, and be an honest, upright man.

" But with the advent of these men my downward course began. The day burns still into my brain when I first came upon them sitting smoking in the verandah of Messrs. Fleecem and Catchem's snuggery. Madeline was in attendance. I had brought her a trinket, a pale blue turquoise coloured necklace, which I thought would suit well her rich, dark beauty. She received me coldly and re-jected my offering. Ah! what I suffered no words of mine could express. I was half mad with misery and jealousy. I knew not what I did.

" I returned to my home on the Miramichi river a soured and desperate man. Shame on me, curses be on my head, for the brutal way in which I afterwards received my poor dear mother's caresses and sympathetic love! I continually upbraided her for our plain, homely existence, and taunted her with the fact that she had impoverished herself and me by paying my father's debts when he died ; I raved at her like the drunken lunatic I was, for I had sought to drown my misery in the degrading remedy of drink. Poor kind old mother! she was too old, too frail, too suffering to bear my brutal excesses ; she took to her bed and died. And I, Lady Maeva, who

should have been beside her, who should
have held her poor dear hand in mine,
and sought to soothe the suffering she was
enduring by gentleness and filial love, at
the moment she passed away, lonely and
unattended, was indulging in noisy drunken
excess.

" The news reached me one day that
she, for the love of whom I had thus
fallen, was to be married to one of these
English visitors. I had ascertained who
they were. One, a pale, sickly-looking
youth of twenty-one, was Ruthven, Earl
of Wrathness; the other was his cousin
and heir-presumptive, Mr. Harold Darrell.
I had ascertained, moreover, that this latter,
who was a fine, handsome young man, was
hopelessly, like myself, head over ears

enamoured of her, and at daggers drawn with his cousin in consequence of his engagement.

But the marriage came off nevertheless. Messrs. Fleecem and Catchem were not the men to allow such a prize to escape them. It was hurried on, and very little engagement time allowed for, and Madeline Dartrey became Lady Wrathness.

" But though she had married him, and Messrs. Fleecem and Catchem had netted a good round sum by the transaction, Lady Wrathness's heart was not in her husband's keeping. I believe she had the greatest loathing for the puny, sallow-faced little fellow, while in her heart she was burning with a consuming passion for his handsome cousin young Harold Darrell.

" Be that as it may, I received one day
a note in her own handwriting in which
she begged me to come and see her. Had
I been any one else but the idiot that I
was, I would have spurned her message
underfoot, and treated it with rigid silence.
But I did not. The passion for that bad
beautiful creature was still upon me. I
cared not on what terms I saw her again,
so that I might see her and be by her
side. Lady Maeva, I obeyed the summons
and I went. Cunning, clever, scheming
woman, she received me with downcast
looks and tears. She feigned a love for
me she never felt, and cast the blame of
her marriage on her so-called guardians.
Dupe that I was, I believed her and
listened to her viper tongue. Mr. Harold

Darrell had mysteriously disappeared up country somewhere, and the ground was free for her intrigue with me.

" She led me on bit by bit. I was mad for the love of her. There was nothing I would not have done at her bidding, and she knew it.

" Lady Maeva, she tested me at last ; she hinted to me the purpose foul she had conceived ; she offered me the price of its reward—her hand. Briefly, she promised me to marry me *if I would do away with him, her husband.* It was about this time that Harold Darrell returned. A sort of patched-up reconciliation took place between the cousins, who became to all appearance friends once more. But there was this about Madeline, she seemed to have the power of fascination upon us all three, and she took good care young Harold should not escape her. It was easy to see he loved her still.

"Ah! do not look at me so with those sad grey eyes of yours, or I shall never be able to finish my tale. It is difficult for hoary sin to face the features of a pure, good life. But, Lady Maeva, I had sold myself to the passion of *my life*, and was doomed. Let me whisper it,—I accepted her terms, nay, with cold-blooded ferocity unfolded to her my plan.

" I bade her on a certain specified night express a wish to obtain a draught of a certain water which is procurable only from a certain spring, which bubbles up in one corner of a certain cave called 'Condean Weegan,' situated in the Indian Reserve, near the Big Hole, on the north-west of Newcastle. This cave can only be reached from the water, and past it the river rushes very rapidly about ten feet below. I told her to address us chaffingly, to invite us all to proceed thither in quest of the desired beverage, and before we started to drink our health all round in wine. I had secretly resolved that the glasses of Lord Wrathness and his cousin should be drugged,—you shall learn wherefore,—and I promised that night to do the deed. She agreed to my proposition, and I laid my plans accordingly. I conveyed to the cave two heavy leaden weights, to which I attached a strong short chain, with a snap collar at the other end, and secreted it close to the entrance.

"The day arrived. We sat at table discussing the evening meal. Suddenly my lady complained of neuralgic pains, and feigned great suffering. 'If you men have a spark of chivalry in you,' she exclaimed, 'you will fetch me a draught of water from the Condean Weegan spring. It is the only remedy I have found yet which assuages these pains.' Simultaneously we all three sprang to our feet. Lord Wrathness and Harold Darrell were heated with the wine which I had drugged. The former asked his cousin, angrily, 'what the devil he wanted to come for. Were not two men enough to fetch a draught of water?' She glanced at Harold, and gave him an encouraging little nod. He replied, hotly, that he intended to go. High words ensued. She interfered and begged them to make peace, and for her sake to go quickly. 'Pledge me,' she cried, 'each of you before you go in one more glass of wine.'

"Poor dupes! they did so. Both of these men loved that woman. She hated one in return. She loved the other passionately, but this at the time I knew not, for I too was her dupe.

"We reached the cave by means of a boat, and swung ourselves upwards by the help of a rope which hung suspended from the interior. The drugged wine was taking effect. Already Harold was stupefying fast, and Wrathness was pretty nearly gone. The former staggered forward into the

cave and sank upon the ground well-nigh
speechless; the latter stood against the
crystal rocks of the interior, striving to
steady himself. Now was my time. I
stole to his side. I am a powerful man,
you see,—he a poor, puny boy. I seized
him by the throat. He strove to cry, to
struggle. His glazed eyes started from
their sockets. I dragged him to the entrance, and dashed his head against the
pointed rocks. Quickly I snapped around
his neck the collar to which was attached
the chain and weights, and hurled him into
the rapid waters below. They closed above
him with a gurgle, and Ruthven, Lord
Wrathness, sleeps beneath the Miramichi
river. Mad with excitement, I rushed into
the inner cave, and dragged the prostrate

Harold from where he lay, letting him down into the boat by means of the cord. Quickly I followed him, and rowed the boat to land. A bright thought had struck me when I first formed my plan. I determined to accuse Harold Darrell with the murder of his cousin.

"How I got him back to the house I never knew. The tale I told on arrival was, that Lord Wrathness had fallen into the river, in a drunken state, from the cave's edge, and, before help could reach him had been swept away, and was drowned. To Madeline I, of course, confided the truth, though, for the matter of that, I had sketched on paper my plan and committed it to words. She had taken possession of this living proof of my guilt, had thoroughly perused it, and knew all.

"Then I claimed from her the price of my foul deed. She put me off with the excuse that, for appearances' sake, I must bide my time a bit, and let her act the part of a mourning widow. I fell into the snare. I waited as she bade me. I woke up one morning to learn that she was the engaged of Harold Darrell, now Earl of Wrathness. In my madness and fury I went to him and accused him of murder. I told him that on that fatal night, drunk with wine and jealousy, the two had quarrelled in the cave. I described to him how he had struck his cousin, and then hurled him into the rushing Miramichi, beneath which the poor lad had sunk to rise no more. I told him that for her sake I held the secret in silence, but that on the day he married her I would denounce him.

" Lady Maeva, he believed me, and to this day he imagines he did the deed, though with no malice aforethought. The next day I received a visit from him, when he offered me a large sum down to observe silence, and a handsome annuity for life if I would leave the country, and be to the world as dead. I accepted, and for this reason.

" After my first interview with him I had gone to her, and, after bitter upbraidings, had sworn to expose Lord Wrathness as the murderer of his cousin. With a cruel laugh she told me that she

held in her possession my carefully prepared plan and minute of the projected
murder. She swore that if I acted thus,
and attempted to prevent her marriage,
she would expose me as the actual
murderer, and bring me to justice.

"She was too many for me, and I
succumbed to her scheming. On receiving
Lord Wrathness's letter I accepted his
offer, and came here. Here I have dwelt
since that fatal day, a miserable, heart-
broken man, with but two objects in life,
the heaping up of gold and revenge.

"I have succeeded in both. Through
my instrumentality he was made aware
of the character of the woman he had
wedded, details of which I shall not
dream of relating to one so young and

pure as you. I had the satisfaction of
seeing his love for her turn to hate, and of
learning that long since he left her, and
refused to live with her as his wife,
giving her an allowance, but otherwise
disowning her. And she in turn now
hates him bitterly, and pursues him with
unrelenting vengeance, while he is para-
lysed with the belief that he is the
murderer of his cousin, and, as such,
seeks to evade the malicious vengeance
of his wife, who he now believes to be
in possession of his secret. I alone am
the unhappy witness of the truth. If I
present myself to declare him innocent,
that woman holds over me the clear,
proven charge, writ in my own hand, of
murder."

CHAPTER XV

SILENCE, drear, dead silence followed upon this fearful avowal of crime. The prematurely aged man sat in exactly the same position, only that his hand closed tighter over his eyes, and his head sank heavier upon that hand. They were a strange pair, those two. One so fallen and so steeped in crime, so almost past redemption in his sullen, heart-broken despair; the other a girl, a mere child, who six months before knew nothing either of love or hate, of passion or jealousy, and much less of murder.

But Maeva, child though she was in

years, had for ever o'erstepped the
boundary-line which separates that tender
age from womanhood. She had grasped
the secret which, old since the world
began, has nerved the heart of woman
to deeds of valorous self-sacrifice and
stupendous daring. For what will not a
woman do or dare for the man she loves?
What was it that prompted this favoured
child of nature, with a world of happiness
before her, with all that hungry humanity
most covets, to fling every thought of
such from her, and to concentrate every
energy and strain every nerve to save
from a hunted life, and perhaps terrible
end, a man who could be nothing to her
in the future? Maeva could answer this
question well. She knew that since that

moment when she found him, in the darkness of night, stretched on that lonely ledge
in the most dreaded spot of the Gleena
Forest, a bleeding, maimed, and helpless
cripple, hovering between life and death
because he had sought to gratify her childish
whim,—she knew that her heart had gone
out to him past recall, and that she loved
him, loved him with a passionate, clinging
love, which can only come once in a
lifetime to any mortal being.

She never paused to ask herself if he
loved her in return. That was no part
of her rigid loyalty and devotion. She
only knew one thing, that was, that she
loved him, and that to save him from
misery and a fearful end she would
willingly give her life.

She sat so still after Richard Emerson had ceased speaking that one might have esteemed her dead or asleep. Her face was very white; she leant back in her chair grasping its two arms tightly, the beautiful eyes closed, the pearly teeth rigidly clenched. In her mind's eye she was reviewing the terrible tale she had heard, and racking her brain for a means of circumventing the relentless and malicious intentions of that woman, who had sworn to track and pursue him to the uttermost ends of the earth till she had brought his proud and haughty spirit to bay. Maeva's mind was made up.

"I see but one way to help Lord Wrathness without betraying you," she said, slowly and distinctly.

He raised his careworn face and looked at her. " And that way ? " he exclaimed eagerly.

" We must get possession of the plan and minute of the murder which you drew up, and which you say is in her keeping."

He laughed drily. " You might as well try to get the moon. You would have about as much chance."

" And yet that is the key to the situation," continued Maeva eagerly. " With that in our possession she would cease to have any hold over you, and could no longer threaten you with exposure, unless you upheld her in her brutal and revengeful purpose. Tell me, Mr. Emerson, have you no shadow of idea where the document is ? "

" I have none whatever," he replied wearily; " would to God I had, I would move heaven and earth to obtain it!"

" Well, it must be got somehow or other," exclaimed Maeva. " Lady Wrathness left for Chili, you said?"

" She went on in the *Valparaiso*, which is bound for Santiago," he replied; " but whether she lands there or not she made no mention to me."

Maeva rose from her seat.

" I can do nothing more here to-day, it appears to me," she said quietly; " but, Mr. Emerson, will you let me say this much? I came to you to-day to learn the truth of this terrible accusation. You offered to sell me all the information you possessed if I would pay for it, and you

named your sum, £10,000. As I pointed
out to you, until I come of age I cannot
pay the money, but I gave you my word
of honour that the moment I did, you
should have it; and moreover I pledged
my word to keep your confession secret.
Both those promises I sacredly swear to
observe; and you have told me that you
trust me."

"I do," he said in a low voice.

"And that trust shall not be mis-
placed," she continued; "and for fear of
my death, I shall leave a written state-
ment and request in regard to the money.
There will be no fear that you will not
get it."

He bowed his head but said nothing.
Maeva made a movement as if to go.

Suddenly she paused. There was a look of intense pity in her eyes as she turned and looked at him.

" Forgive me," she said gently, " but oh ! Mr. Emerson, will you not pray to God, whose name you mentioned just now, and ask Him to pardon you and help you to repent ? Do not let this terrible crime drag you lower and lower in despair, until you cease to know what hope, repentance, and forgiveness mean. Will you try and remember what your poor old mother taught you once ? Will you strive to atone for your terrible past ? "

He raised his head and looked at her with a wild, haggard expression. There was a gleam of mockery in his sunken eyes, a withering smile on his thin, pinched lips.

As Maeva sadly eyed him, she could hardly bring herself to believe that he was only forty-two. He had all the appearance of a man past sixty.

"Child," he cried, "you know not what you ask. It is impossible. I cannot pray to a God I do not believe in, or ask forgiveness where I hope for none. To sink lower than I have aleady is not possible. Have I not reached the lowest abyss of infamy now? Do not, I charge you, mention my mother's name ; it is dead to me for eternity. I have no hope left to me now. I live for but two things, as I have told you—revenge and gold. Leave me." He ceased speaking. The silvering head sank down upon his arms outstretched upon the table, and the miserable, fallen, hopeless man burst into a terrible fit of weeping.

She stared at him in a bewildered way. His words had struck her with a strange dread. She felt that between her and this man an abyss of terrible depth lay, separating their natures and very existence. Very silently and softly the girl withdrew. As she passed along the corridor to the front door the trickling of the fountain was the only sound that broke the stillness of that quiet house, save one, and that was the sad, despairing sobs of the lonely, unbelieving, unrepentant murderer. With a shudder she turned the handle of the door and passed out into the streets of Rio. Esca was walking slowly up and down outside. He looked at her eagerly as she came to meet him.

"Well, good news, I hope?"

She laid her hand upon his arm.

"Yes, I have good news," she said. "Esca, I cannot tell you all I have heard to-day, because I am pledged to secrecy. But I can tell you this much. Lord Wrathness did not murder his cousin. The man who did it is alive, and Lady Wrathness holds written proof of his guilt. But if Lord Wrathness is to be saved that written proof must be obtained."

"Whew-w-w!" he whistled; "will that be possible?"

"It must be!" she exclaimed passionately; "it must be even if I die in getting it."

He smiled. "No, Maeva," he said very gently, "if it is possible to get it, and it be God's will, I will get it for you ; but if any one is to die in obtaining it, that person shall be myself."

She started. His words seemed to let a flood of light into her brain. She looked up at him with beseeching eyes.

" Oh ! do not talk like that, dear Esca ; many a true word is spoken in jest. It would break my heart if any harm came to you through your unselfish, generous friendship for me."

He did not answer her. The boy with the fair, manly face, blue eyes, and yellow-gold, clustering hair was looking out over the blue bay of Rio Harbour, away beyond, on the gorgeous tropical girt hills. He was thinking that his would be a happy death indeed, if by it he purchased happiness for her; that his reward would be sweet beyond measure if she were to mourn his loss.

They were turning into the old market-place again, redolent with the odour of many and varied fruits. There was a good sprinkling of naval officers about the place, all intent on the purchases they were mak-ing. As the midshipman and his girl-friend passed through it they came upon Ronald and several other mids, in fits of laughter over the antics of various small monkeys, who were grinning, and fighting, and grimacing in a big cage within which they were confined.

"Oh, Esca, Maeva, do come here!" sang out Ronald, on perceiving them. "Did you, either of you, ever see such ducks as these monkeys are? Stanley,

Cresswell, and I have been in agonies of laughter. These apes are enough to kill one altogether."

" I say, Hamilton, have you heard the news ?" inquired young Stanley, turning to Esca ; and as this latter shook his head and looked at the mid inquiringly that jubilant young officer continued,—

" Why, the corvette *Dauntless* has received the Admiral's orders to take a cruise right round the coast of South America, under dear old Captain Rose ; and she's to carry, besides the first lieutenant, four others, four subs, and eight of us mids. Who do you think these latter are ? Why, you, Angus, I, Graham, Douglas, Percy, Cresswell, and Stanford. Ain't it rare good luck ? Won't we have a pot of fun, my boy ? "

" Thank God!" Esca heard Maeva fervently exclaim; and as he looked at her she whispered in a low voice, " Then we shall not be separated, for I am going to ask my father to go that way too."

He flushed with pleasure. So his presence *was* a comfort to her really. He was of some use to her. Oh! how happy the thought made him. But he only said, addressing himself to Stanley, " I *am* glad. It *will* be ripping."

And Maeva, as she looked at the monkeys to please Ronald, and laughed with him and his middy friends over their squabblings and antics, was revolving in her mind a multitude of things, and framing plans for the future. In those happy August and earlier September days, when

she had sat with Lord Wrathness discussing the coming voyage round the world,
he had often described to her spots and
scenes which he had come across in former
wanderings, and which he had promised to
show her in the travels to come; for it
must be remembered that he was to have
formed one of the *Firefly* party. And she
remembered how he had described to her
the lonely, vast-extending pampas of Patagonia, where it was possible to ride for
hundreds of miles without meeting a single
human being, and that in those regions
only had he experienced the peculiar feeling
of being utterly and entirely alone. And
Maeva and he had discussed this strange,
lonely land often together, and she had
frequently expressed a wish in his presence

to make it one of the very first places to be visited by the *Firefly*.

" He is sure to go there," she said to herself; " and that dreadful woman will miss him if she goes on to Chili in the *Valparaiso*. Oh! how I do hope he has landed in Patagonia."

She had determined to ask her father to let the yacht take the same course as the corvette *Dauntless* was directed to cruise on. There would be nothing strange in this request, as it was but natural that she should wish to see as much of Ronald as possible, and the route was all in order for a voyage round the world. The *Firefly* party were all expected back in three days, and it would be very easy to arrange to leave Rio the same day as the corvette.

As she and Esca walked on to the landing-stage, where one of the yacht's boats was awaiting them, she told him her plans. He listened to them with delight.

" I hope Lord Ettrick and Captain Rose will be able to hit it off between them, though, in such a manner that the *Dauntless* and *Firefly* will stop at the same places," he remarked, a little anxiously. " It would be awful hard lines if we got separated. Do ask Lord Ettrick to try and keep with us, won't you, Maeva ? "

" That is just what I intend to ask him, Esca," she replied, quietly. " Leave that to me, I think I shall be able to manage it all right."

They were nearing the *Bucephalus* as she spoke. Esca looked at his watch.

"My time's almost up now," he remarked. "I've got to go on duty in half an hour. Can you put me on board, please? I shall not be able to go on with you to the yacht. I shall see you, however, again to-night, as Ronald has asked me to dine there, and we have both got leave to come."

She was steering, and at once turned the boat's nose for the ironclad, which loomed ahead like an enormous monster of the deep, rearing itself above the placid waters of the harbour, that day undisturbed by a single current of air. Half-a-dozen powerful strokes from the four stalwart sailors that rowed the boat brought them well-nigh to the *Bucephalus*. In a clear, ringing voice she gave the order to ship oars, and brought the boat round with a neat curve alongside the landing-place. Esca, who was standing up, sprang out.

"Au revoir!" he exclaimed, holding out his hand and leaning down to where she sat. "We shall meet again this evening. Look out for Ronald and me about half-past six or a quarter to seven. We'll come the earliest we can, you bet."

She smiled as she took his hand. She thought she had never seen him look so handsome before. The flush of perfect health was on his fair face, his blue eyes looked so kind and winning, his yellow-gold hair, ruffled by the action of taking off his cap, played about his forehead in clustering curls, those curls which had been his fond and loving mother's delight and pride, and which he would often laughingly term " obstreperous monkeys," when they frequently wandered outside the region of strict neatness. Yes, he looked handsome indeed, as he stood there in the prime of his boyhood and youth, a boyhood which had been singularly noble and pure, a youth in whom all the promise of boyhood shone forth conspicuously bright. His was a nature which none could do otherwise but love, so generous, impulsive, truthful, gentle, and kind. Yes, Esca indeed looked handsome as he stood there, waving a smiling adieu, and the picture was one which Maeva, who looked upon it then, never from that day could forget.

It came back to her long afterwards, when he was no longer by to cheer her with kindly hope and boyish honest counsel.

It came back to her when the sand of time, running its course, swiftly, surely, with no returning wave, spoke to her of days that could never come again. It came back to her in her dreams, when in restless sleep she seemed to hold communion with her boy-friend, as in those vanished days. It came back to her in many a sudden memory that would rise involuntarily, all unbidden to her mind, of that brave, generous, boyish, noble heart, that had beat with such loyal, enthusiastic devotion— for her, the first and the last love of his young life.

CHAPTER XVI.

"WHAT place do you call this, Captain Leportier?" inquired a tall dark-haired man, who, arrayed in a mackintosh and sou'wester, had been pacing up and down the deck of the Pacific Steam Navigation Company's liner the *Valparaiso*, as, amidst a squall of hail, rain, wind, and spray, it dropped anchor well on in the afternoon in the Straits of Magellan, opposite and about a mile distant from a long, low-stretching, sandy shore, upon which the surf beat with relentless fury.

"Puntas Arenas, otherwise Sandy Point,"

answered the officer addressed, in a brisk voice; adding, "we are going to try and get the mails off if it is possible, but it is blowing pretty hard, and we shall have a job, I expect, to do so."

"I suppose you cannot get this big vessel any nearer the shore with safety?" inquired the man of the captain again.

"Shouldn't like to try," observed that individual drily, "unless I wanted to forfeit my post and lose my ship into the bargain."

"There's a yacht braced up and lying pretty close to the shore," observed the man, as he unslung a binocular from his shoulder and looked carefully through the glasses. "Can you make out who she is, captain?" he added, handing that officer the binocula.

"Yes," answered Captain Leportier slowly, as he took a survey of the anchored craft, that lay about half a mile distant from the *Valparaiso;* "I've often seen her before, she's no stranger to these seas. Her name's the *Mayflower*, and her owner is the Earl of Wrathness. I believe he's a regular globe-trotter, been all over the world."

"The *Mayflower!*" exclaimed the man, hastily seizing the glasses which the captain was handing him back as he spoke, and looking eagerly through them. "Are you sure it is, captain?"

"As sure as I am that this is the *Valparaiso*," responded the captain, a little impatiently. "Hey! Mr. Charlton," he called out to the first officer, who was on the bridge, "better let them have a little powder there on shore, and hurry them up. We can't stay here all day."

"Aye, aye, sir," sang out the individual addressed, a smart type of the mercantile marine officer. The next moment the good ship reverberated from stem to stern, as the gallant wee nine-pounder belched forth its smoky and noisy message to the half dead-alive inhabitants of Puntas Arenas.

"They're launching the surf-boat now, sir," called out Mr. Charlton from the bridge, who had been watching through his glasses the effect of the nine-pounder's message. "Mails up, men, there—look alive!"

"Aye, aye, sir," responded several voices.

"I think I shall bid you good-bye here, Captain," observed the man who had been hitherto addressing him. " I should not like to pass Patagonia without having a look at the country, and I suppose one of your liners will soon be passing again, eh ? "

" Every fortnight," ejaculated the captain shortly. He had not taken a liking to this passenger somehow, and treated him with mere frigid politeness. In his heart he was not sorry that the individual in question was taking himself off.

The man said no more, but went below. A quarter of an hour later he came on deck again, carrying what had the appearance of a small black business bag ; while one of the stewards followed him bearing a neat portmanteau, a gun, rifle, cartridge-case, and bundle of rugs.

These he set down on the deck close to the companion ladder. Judging by his obsequious behaviour, the owner of these articles had given him a handsome tip. The surf-boat was slowly nearing the *Valparaiso*, half-enveloped from time to time in clouds of spray, which the shrieking squalls hurled over the flat-bottomed craft with ungovernable fury. There were four oars in the boat, each manned by two men, who were pulling with all their might and main against the waves and sudden blasts, that made rowing anything but child's work. A ninth man was at the helm, and a tenth standing up in the bows, with a coil of rope all ready to throw on board.

"Now, Mr. Darrell ; sorry to hurry you,

sir, but you'll have to look sharp if you want to board that old tub without getting a dousing," exclaimed the captain, coming up to the passenger's side as he stood watching the surf-boat's approach.

" Very good, captain," he answered coolly, " I'm not green at that sort of work ; if you'll guarantee my luggage gets in, I'll guarantee myself gets in safe enough."

" That's a bargain," observed the officer.

The tub, as it had been irreverently called by the captain, had reached the ship's stern, and with a magnificent cast aloft the man in the bows had sent the rope with unerring aim into the hands of several sailors, who stood ready to grasp and make it tight to the ship. By this

time wind and current had drifted it in a
line with the ladder, and as it heaved
upwards to the deck the mails were trans-
ferred with extraordinary rapidity to its
interior. Alive and alert the sailors had
to be, as a moment too late or a moment
too soon, would have enveloped the precious bags in the stormy waters, as the
surf boat sank into the trough of the
sea.

"Everything in, lads?" inquired the
first officer cheerily of the men as he
descended from his perch aloft.

"Everything, sir," they responded
promptly.

"And this gentleman's luggage, eh?"

"Aye, aye, sir; stowed away all safe."

"Then good-bye, Captain Leportier,"

said Mr. Darrell, holding out his hand to
that officer.

" But stay, sir, we must let you in with
a rope," called out the first officer warn-
ingly.

" Here, Stoker, passenger's rope—sharp."

" No need," observed the passenger
quietly, as after having shaken the captain's hand he stepped back a few paces.
The next moment he had run forward,
leapt lightly on to the rail, and balancing
himself to a nicety had dropped into the
stern of the surf boat as it rose on a
more than usually excitable wave.

" By Jove, that was neatly done!" exclaimed Mr. Charlton to the captain; " the
man gave me quite a turn at first. I
thought he was going to commit suicide."

"He looks evil enough for anything," responded Captain Leportier, with a shrug of the shoulders; "I never saw a face I liked less."

"Handsome enough to please most people," suggested Mr. Charlton with a smile.

"Yes, with the beautiful expression of a fallen angel, Charlton. Take my word for it,—I'm a bit of a character reader, and I tell you that man's a bad 'un."

"Well, he's off now," observed the first officer, with a laugh. "I daresay you're right, sir; you generally are."

"Well, there's nothing to keep us now. No use dawdling here. Weigh anchor and let's be off, Charlton," observed the commander hastily, as if anxious to change the conversation, and at the same time moving towards the bridge.

" Aye, aye, sir."

Up came the anchor quickly from its watery bed. Round went the screw with tremendous velocity. Soon the old *Valparaiso* was at full speed, and steaming rapidly for Cape Horn. Mr. Ruys Darrell, or, as we may also call that personage, Lady Wrathness,—for it was no other, —stood watching its disappearance from the rickety old tumbledown pier which was all Sandy Point could boast of, and elevated from the water but a few yards. " It's lucky I did not go on in her," she muttered, as the big looming ship disappeared in the misty and squall-shrouded distance; " it was lucky I caught sight of

my lord's skulking *Mayflower* when I did.
Fate is working in my favour.   I never
thought to track him as quickly as this.
He thought he had escaped me, and that
big-eyed child at Rio thinks him safe.
Ha, ha, ha!" and she laughed a mocking,
derisive laugh.

" Mister want lodging ?   Shall me carry
his things for him ? " inquired a sallow,
nondescript creature of the half-breed type,
touching his greasy cap.

" Yes," answered the soliloquiser in
response ; " show me where I can get a
room and something to eat."

" Mister foller me," said the half-breed
glibly, as he shouldered the portmanteau,
tucked gun and rifle under one arm, and
seized with his left hand the cartridge-

case and roll of rugs. He even made
an attempt to possess himself of the black
business bag which Lady Wrathness carried in her hand, but she waved him off.

" No, leave it," she said, " I will carry
this myself."

Her guide led the way up the only
street which the settlement contained, a
broad, sandy tract lined on each side by
a row of unevenly built wooden houses,
huts, and shanties. There were very few
people to be seen in this deserted looking street; a child or two sprawled in
the sand; a Chilian soldier strutted along
with an air of importance ill becoming
his appearance or the place; a hound
here and there yelped or snarled an
angry greeting. Everything looked what

the place was—a miserable, dead-alive convict settlement. The half-bred nondescript did not proceed very far, for turning suddenly to the right he brought himself up at the entrance of a square logwood-built house of better appearance than most of the other buildings. A swarthy Gaucho Indian lay stretched out on the sand in a state of semi-intoxication, and at his feet lay curled up two black, wiry-looking dogs, a cross between the Scotch deerhound and African greyhound.

" Pedro ! " shouted the nondescript in a cracked guttural voice.

A man with a Spanish face answered the call. " This mister want lodging, food," explained the nondescript, pointing to Lady Wrathness, who stood just behind him.

"Vous parlez français, monsieur?" inquired Pedro, addressing himself to her with a low bow.

"Pas bien," she responded; "but you can speak English, cannot you?"

"Veray leetle," he replied diffidently, "but p'raps 'nough make myself understan'."

"Can you give me a room of some sort?" she asked him next; "I must have one to myself."

"This only a store, but there is empty room upstairs; if monsieur like make shake-down there. I can give monsieur bread, meat, beer, brandy, or kania."

"Show me the room then, and take me up some bread, meat, and a bottle of brandy there," she answered quickly ; "and here, you man, bring up my luggage."

The nondescript made haste to obey, and Lady Wrathness following the two men up a narrow wooden staircase found herself in a small empty room with a tiny window in it. There was absolutely not a shred of furniture of any kind, not so much as a chair or table, much less a bed. She handed the nondescript a silver coin ; he seized it like a wild beast, and rushing down the staircase began shouting to Pedro to give him some kania.

Lady Wrathness heard him, and asked her landlord what kania was.

" A hot drink," he replied, " stronger than brandy ; Arius soon drunk now."

" Well. go and give him his kania," she

answered with a laugh, "and bring me my brandy."

" Monsieur will be served in a moment," he replied, as he vanished downstairs.

Left to herself, Lady Wrathness opened the black bag, which had never quitted her hands since she left the *Valparaiso*, and peering inside smiled.

" Safe," she muttered, " safe as a door-nail. It would not do to lose you, would it ? Without you I should be a helpless cripple in my path of vengeance ; without you that skulking husband of mine would be able to snap his fingers in my face. Ah! but I have you safe, and I will never let you from my grasp ; if I lost you I might as well be dead."

She broke off abruptly, for Pedro was

ascending the stairs. He entered the next moment bringing a loaf of bread, a knife, two cold chops, and a bottle of brandy, together with a glass and a jug of water. These he set down on the floor, brought some salt out of his pocket in a dirty piece of paper, and with the remark " Monsieur est servi," left the apartment.

Lady Wrathness felt in her pocket and brought out a knife, in a recess of which nestled a corkscrew. This latter she quickly opened, screwed it into the brandy bottle's cork, and drew it out hastily. The next moment she had filled the glass half-full with that raw liquid, and raising it to her lips had tossed it off.

She smacked them together with relish as the burning fluid trickled down her throat. She felt it circulating through her body, filling her veins with a strange electric fire. The dull, miserable room looked bright enough in her eyes now, all was *couleur de rose*. She looked at the bread and cold chops and salt lying in the dirty paper at her feet, and spurned them with a movement of disgust. She looked at the bottle with its rich, golden-brown liquid therein, and bending down poured out yet another draught, which she tossed off in the same way as she had done the first.

She was ready for anything now. Her brain was on fire, yet she had sense enough about her to undo her rugs and lay them out in a corner of her room. The portmanteau she placed close by, the gun, rifle, and cartridge-case alongside, and the precious black bag exactly where she could hold it with her hands when lying down.

" I am tired," she muttered ; " better to have a sleep before I decide on anything. I can see my lord to-morrow."

There was a triumphant ring in her voice. She had run the hunted quarry to bay, and could bide her time for its destruction. So at least thought Lady Wrathness, as she threw herself on her hard couch in a semi-unconscious state, and closed her dark, gleaming, and wicked eyes. With her hands close clutching the black business bag, this woman, scheming, bad, revengeful, with the hell-fire water burning within her, sank into a heavy but restless slumber. Often during the dark, lonely night she would spring up into a sitting posture, and clutching wildly in front of her cry out in fear and horror, while beads of sweat sprang sparkling upon her dark terror-stricken features as she endured her fearful dreams.

She dreamed that he stood beside her, that tall, handsome, sad-eyed man, whose life she had sought to ruin and turn into a desert. She dreamt that she, knife in hand, was attempting to spring upon him and stab him in the heart, but that ever as she strove to reach him he vanished from her sight, only to appear again, pale, melancholy, and reproachful. She dreamed that by a superhuman effort she had grasped him at last, and that the knife was poised ready to strike him down. But even as it flashed through the air she heard a cry full of intense pathos and yearning, her hand was struck up, the blade flew from her grasp, a torrent of rushing blood poured down upon her. It overpowered and overwhelmed her; she felt it choking the life from her body. She strove to free herself from its weight. In vain. Down, down, she sank beneath that ocean of gory foam, lost beyond hope, beyond the possibility of rescue. With a cry of fearful terror Lady Wrathness sprang up from where she lay. The sun was streaming into the cheerless room, the bread, cold meat, and salt lay untouched upon the floor. By her side lay the brandy-bottle, overturned on its side, the liquid having streamed out in a long, pear-shaped pool upon the boards. What an awakening!

" Is the gentleman on his yacht now ? " she inquired a few hours later of Pedro, the storekeeper.

" But no, monsieur, he gone into pampas, hunting."

She ground her teeth.

" Can I get horses and a guide here ? " she said eagerly.

" But yes, monsieur. There is Gregorio, the best guide in all the country round. He have horses, dogs, he know the pampas well."

Two hours later, and a small cavalcade rode out of the sandy, cheerless settlement of Sandy Point. The cavalcade consisted of ten loose horses, three wiry-looking dogs, and three mounted horsemen. One of these was Gregorio, the Gaucho Indian; the other Arius, the nondescript; the third Mr. Ruys Darrell, otherwise Lady Wrathness. They were bound for the pampas of Patagonia.

CHAPTER XVII

MESSRS. Fleecem and Catchem sat in their business-room in No. 6, Furnival Square, and obsequiously facing them stood the Co., with smiling visage, and washing his hands with invisible soap. We have seen Mr. Fleecem before. Mr. Catchem & Co. have hitherto not been introduced to the reader.

Mr. Catchem was very unlike Mr. Fleecem. He was tall and spare, with a meagre, sallow face, large hands, and lugubrious expression. He rarely smiled, and when he did, it was lugubriously; certainly not within the memory of business men had he been heard to laugh. He dressed in black, had high stand-up collars, and wore a ring on his first finger. In business transactions Mr. Catchem was unmatched; he knew his work to a T. No one had ever got six to four the better of Mr. Catchem, but this gentleman had frequently got six to four the better of other people. He lived for one thing—making money. In pursuit of that hobby he was not particular what he did or how he acted, so long as the card turned up was trumps. Messrs. Fleecem and Catchem were a nice pair!

The Co. was a cringing, oily man, willing to do any amount of dirty work so that it advanced the interests of the firm of Fleecem, Catchem, & Co. As his soubriquet implied, he had an interest in this firm's advancement, and he knew that there was no better way to accomplish this than by following out the dictates of the two senior partners. In selecting their 'Co. Messrs. Fleecem and Catchem had acted with their usual discrimination.

" Say we are out, Rawton," Mr. Fleecem was saying, at the time this chapter opens. " Say we are not expected back to-day. Say the capital must be paid back sharp to time, and the interest every penny down, or we must act as we have said. Can't possibly extend the time. Land is falling in value ; we must strike while the iron is hot, if we are to turn an honest penny by this transaction. Of course you needn't mention this last remark, I need hardly tell you, Rawton," concluded the smart lawyer with a laugh.

" Oh! of course not, Mr. Fleecem. Rely upon me to say the right thing. Shall I go to her ladyship now?"

"Well, yes, Rawton, I think you had better. Won't do to keep her too long, you know. And mind you're careful. She's a deuced clever woman, remember. Has business matters at the end of her finger nails. I'd rather face a dozen like her husband than one of herself. Eh, Catchem?" and Mr. Fleecem laughed again.

" Yes," assented Catchem, looking lugu-briously in front of him, " she is *very* clever. Rawton, you must be *very* careful."

" I will," answered that individual, and then he turned and left the room.

He passed down a narrow corridor and opened the door of Mr. Fleecem's snuggery, the same which has been introduced to the reader in a former chapter. Standing looking out of the window at the gloomy aspect of Furnival Square was a slight, neatly-dressed lady, with a girlish figure, and of medium height. As the door opened she turned round, bowed slightly, and with an inquiring expression said,—

" Mr. Fleecem ? "

" No, madam, I regret to say that both Mr. Fleecem and Mr. Catchem are away out of town. Not expected back till to-morrow," answered the oily Mr. Rawton, with a smile and a wriggle.

" I am sorry for that ; I particularly wanted to see Mr. Fleecem," she observed, with a shade of annoyance in her tone.

" I hope, Lady Plunger, I may do as well as Mr. Fleecem ; I am really as perfectly acquainted with the matter in which you and Sir Beaufort are interested as my partner, and can discuss it with you fully, if that is what you wish."

" Hardly," she answered, and there was a pathetic ring in her voice. " I came in the hope of seeing Mr. Fleecem, and inducing him to give us a few months longer, in which to get the money to meet the interest and pay off the loan. Cannot you give me any hope that your partners will agree to this ? "

" I fear not, madam. The lenders have

called their money in, and if it is not paid
by the date specified, Mr. Fleecem and
Mr. Catchem will have no alternative but
to put Boswell Towers and property, up
for sale."

"But do you know what this means to
us, sir? Since the mortgage was put on
the property, land has been going down fast
in value, and if you sell the dear old home
now, it is just as likely as not, to fetch
about enough to pay off the mortgagees
and leave no margin for us. This will
mean ruin."

"Madam, in a matter of business we
can only look at it from one point of view.
No one will regret more than my partners
the inconvenience you and Sir Beaufort may
be put to, but you see it cannot be helped."

"Ah, sir, if but time could be given us, I feel sure I and Sir Beaufort could pay the money off, if you would re-consider this crushing interest you are charging. It is too heavy, and now I understand compound interest is being charged."

"It is," replied Mr. Rawton, with a smile. "Mr. Fleecem and Mr. Catchem always have made it a rule to charge compound interest on loans, when the payments due thereon, are not paid up punctually. We have no alternative."

She looked at him with a contemptuous expression on her anxious, intelligent face. She saw that there was neither mercy nor pity to expect in that direction, that to plead would be waste of time, to appeal to the heart worse than useless. She rose

up from the seat on which she had sat
herself down after Mr. Rawton had entered
the room.

" I am to understand then, that your
partners and yourself refuse to give my
husband time? That in fact you mean to
ruin us?"

" My dear madam, pray do not put it
in that light," said the oily Co., diffidently.

" Truth is the best light in which to see
all things," she replied scornfully. She
was thinking of the beautiful old home
in the Midlands, the dearly loved hunters,
the splendid kennel of setters, and of the
old scenes and spots in and around Boswell
Towers, where she and Sir Beaufort had
spent many a happy day together, until
the demon gambling took him away from

her. She was thinking how all these would have to be parted with, and a farewell for good made to the old favourite haunts. She was thinking of the terrible struggle there would be to meet all the debts faithfully, and the weary labour of winding everything up. And then her thoughts flew onward to that dark future, when poverty would stare them in the face, and trouble, black trouble, would hang above them like a pall.

" If it was only myself, I could face it, I would not mind it, I could work for my living," she cried half aloud; " but there are the boys, poor little chaps, and Beaufort Oh! how will he ever bear it?"

She checked herself; she saw the Co.'s eyes fixed upon her. Pride came to her assistance. In a cold, matter-of-fact voice she inquired, " Can you give me the date when the place will be put up?"

" I think we wrote Sir Beaufort, madam, that it would be in six weeks from this."

" Thank you," she said quietly. " Good-morning." She passed him with a sneer on her lips, and never so much as looked at him. In another moment her hand was on the door, and she was walking along the corridor to the entrance. A neat brougham stood waiting; she ran quickly down the steps, opened the door, and as she closed it on herself, called out to the coachman:

" Home."

He touched his hat, then his horse, a fine blood bay, and the brougham quickly rattled out of Furnival Square.

It made its way through a good many intricate streets and turnings, but the coachman knew his whereabouts well, and in fifteen minutes from the time of leaving Furnival Square it had pulled up in front of its destination, a smart house in Albemarle Street.

"I shall not want you any more to-day, Moss," said Lady Plunger, as she stepped out of the brougham, "but come in for orders about five o'clock."

"Very good, my lady."

She rang the house bell, the door was opened with alacrity; the brougham drove off as she entered.

"Where is Sir Beaufort?" she inquired of the butler.

"In the smoking-room, my lady,' answered

that portly individual, breathing hard. He had just been having a cup of soup and glass of wine, along with the lady's maid and housekeeper, in *the room* downstairs, and was considerably puffed by his hasty ascent from below.

The smoking-room was on the ground floor. Lady Plunger passed on to it, opened the door, and entered the room, closing the door softly behind her.

Sir Beaufort was seated by the fire, his face in his hands. A half-finished brandy and soda, and an extinct half-smoked cigarette beside it, stood on a little table close by.

He did not move as his wife entered. She went close up to him, sat herself down on one of the arms of the armchair in which he was seated, and put her right arm round his neck.

" Beaufort dear," she whispered.

He looked up wearily. His face was flushed, his eyes bloodshot and distressed. She could see plainly he had been drinking.

" Well, what do you want ? " he inquired, peevishly ; " don't bother, I'm not up to much just now."

She kissed him gently. " Don't drink any more at present, Beaufort, that's a good boy,—please don't. You've had quite enough, dear old chap. Let me take this horrid stuff away." She had risen as she spoke and laid her hand on the half-empty soda-water glass. He jumped up with an oath.

" I'm blowed if I'm going to be done

out of my drink!" he exclaimed angrily; "let it be, Glorie, do you hear?"

"Oh! all right, Beaufort, drink away," she said, bitterly; "but you can't go on like this, you know. If it had not been for that foul stuff, we should never have been in the terrible position we are now. Beaufort, I must have a talk to you. Do you realise what Messrs. Fleecem and Catchem intend to do?"

"What the devil's that to you?" he said, hotly.

"Everything," she said, sadly, knowing well how the whole brunt of suffering and worry would eventually fall upon herself.

"But, Beaufort dear, do you realise that Boswell Towers is to be put up for auction in six weeks? It will never fetch its worth in the present terrible depreciation of land ; and this being so, after the mortgagees have been paid off there will be little left for us. We owe a great deal. How are all the bills to be paid, and even if we do manage to clear them, what will there be left for us to live on ? "

" Boswell Towers put up for auction, Glorie! Are you mad ? As if I would allow the dear old place to be sold!" he exclaimed, contemptuously.

"Oh! Beaufort, dear, don't trifle like that," she said, wearily. " I have just seen Messrs. Fleecem and Catchem's partner, and he says that if the loan you borrowed from them six months ago, with the interest owing, is not paid up to date, that is to say in five days from now, that the place will be put up for sale in six weeks."

He stared at her and laughed.

" It is no laughing matter, Beaufort ; for we shall be utterly ruined. Instead of thousands a year to spend, as you have been accustomed to, you will have only a few hundreds. We shall have to part with everything, the horses, dogs, servants, the box at Melton, and go and live quietly in some little place with one or two servants only. The boys will have to give up all thought of Eton now, and come home. Not that I mind that though, I can teach them myself."

" Live in a cottage—hundreds a year, Glorie ? Certainly you are gone clean cracked. To begin with, Boswell Towers sha'n't be sold; and secondly, if it was —not that it shall be—it is worth, and would fetch, hundreds of thousands."

"No," she answered firmly, "if it is sold now it would not. It may realise enough to pay off the mortgages on it, but no more. I have been telling you for the last year that you were exceeding your income considerably, and that Mr. Symonds could not possibly keep the banking account going and meet all the interests due on the mortgages as well, and since you raised that £68,000 at twenty per cent., it has become simply impossible to pay the interest on it. You know, dear, you never will look into your estate affairs, so you do not realise the muddle they are in. Well, the climax has

come. Be a man and face it. I will do
all I can to save you bother and worry,
but you must face your position. Let us
work tooth and nail to pay every debt off.
If we can manage that, the disaster will
not be so hard to bear."

"Boswell Towers sha'n't be sold!" he
shouted, stamping his foot, and pulling
the bell violently. "I'll go and see
Fleecem at once. Fleecem's a rare good
chap. Of course you don't know how to
manage him. Never saw a woman yet
who could do business of any sort. Here,
Edward, call a hansom," he continued, as
the footman answered the bell.

"Yes, Sir Beaufort."

Lady Plunger said nothing. She felt
that it was just as well that her husband

should call and see Mr. Fleecem, and be brought face to face with facts at once; so she interposed no objection.

The footman re-appeared.

" The hansom is at the door, Sir Beaufort."

" All right, Edward, get me my hat, stick, and gloves, put them in the hall, and call Stokes. Look sharp!" said the baronet, as he pulled out a cigarette and lit it. Then he turned to his wife.

" Ta-ta, Glorie! Shall be back for dinner, not before. Good-bye, old girl; sorry I was cross,—you won't mind, will you ?"

He put his hands on her shoulders and kissed her; she laid a hand on his arm.

" Oh no, Beaufort! I don't mind. I

know you never mean half you say. But,
dear, do try and think over what I
have told you ; and remember, you've
got a friend here when those whom you
now believe are your friends begin to turn
the cold shoulder on you. It won't be
long coming."

He laughed lightly. The brandy made
trouble seem nothing. The next moment
he was gone.

She sighed as she sat herself down in
his empty chair and looked into the fire.
She felt very sad and weary. So the
bright, gay life she had been leading
was all to come to an end, and in its
place black poverty and weary, hopeless
struggling to make ends meet. Glorie
Plunger had hitherto led a dashing,

brilliant life. She did most things well, was a great favourite in society, gave pleasant parties, had the best men around her, and went to all the best places. Many a man had loved Glorie Plunger, both before and after her marriage; not that she was a coquette, or trifled with their affections, but Glorie was attractive to men, and they fell in love with her accordingly.

As she sat looking into the fire and trying to imagine what the future would be like, she found herself asking the question, somewhat sneeringly, as to how many of these fashionable friends and lovers, would care for her in her straitened circumstances; and then she laughed a bitter, contemptuous laugh as she answered that question in the one word, " Few."

She sat on by the fire, making plans and good resolutions, and endeavouring to reckon up mentally all the payments that would have to be made, the expenses that would have to be put down, and the amount which she and her husband and two boys would in the hard future have to subsist upon. The hours flew by; she did not go in to luncheon. It remained untasted on the table. Suddenly the door-bell rang. There were hurried footsteps in the hall. The smoking-room door was roughly opened and banged to, admitting Sir Beaufort. He looked wild and desperate; there was a haggard, despairing expression about his eyes. Glorie sprang up and ran to meet him.

" Beaufort, dear, what is it ? " she exclaimed anxiously.

" God ! God help me ! " he cried. " Oh ! Glorie, we *are* ruined. Boswell, dear old Boswell, is going to be taken from me. It will break my heart. Ah ! can nothing be done to save the old home ? "

She put her arms round his neck and tried to soothe him, as he burst into a passionate fit of weeping.

CHAPTER XVIII

"AVESTRUZ, Avestruz, choo, choo, La Plata, Sultan, La Liona!" shouted a young man, in a French accent, as he took off his cap and waved it to three great ostrich hounds that were trotting in the rear of the wiry black horse that he rode; at the same time catching hold of the horse's head by drawing the rein tight. At once the animal broke into a gallop, the hounds pricked up their ears, dashed forward, and in another moment were racing along with great raking strides in the wake of a swiftly-fleeing bundle of grey feathers, the ostrich of the Patagonian pampas, whom François Delacroix, the smartest ostrich-hunter in all the plains around, had designated to his dogs as Avestruz.

At the same time a distant view-holloa came floating across the plain, and three mounted horses could be observed bearing down upon the luckless bird. It was a plucky quarry, however, was this swift-footed denizen of the arid plain. Away it dashed with most marvellous rapidity, leaving horses and hounds far in the rear. A low range of hillocky ground ran north-wards about a mile distant, and towards this the fleeting ostrich pointed. Straining every nerve, bending every sinew, in his struggles to lessen the distance between himself and the bird, La Plata, a coal-black, sleek-coated greyhound, in whose veins commingled the blood of the English and African species of that name, was gradually drawing ahead of Sultan and La Liona. Now Sultan was a black-and-white hound of the Indian lurcher breed, with a rough coat, and not a quarter the speed of La Plata. But La Liona, a yellow, rough-coated bitch, a cross between the Scotch deerhound and greyhound, showed evidence that neither pluck nor determination was wanting in her sturdy racing form, though she could not emulate the splendid speed of her black *confrère*.

They had settled down into a racing pace. François, standing up and leaning well forward in his stirrups, sent forth note after note of encouragement to his straining hounds, and close beside him the three other mounted horses galloped well in line. Their riders could be recognised at a glance, for they were no other than Maeva, Ronald, and Esca.

It may be as well to explain that the *Firefly* and *Dauntless* had steamed out of Rio Harbour in each other's company, and after cruising along the coasts of Parana, the Rio Grande do Sul, Uruguay, and Buenos Ayres, whence expeditions had been made up the rivers Plata and Parana into the interior, both ships had brought up at El Carmen, or Patagones, one of the few settlements, and the only one of any size, on the Patagonian coast. Here, at Maeva's earnest request, Lord Ettrick had chartered the services of several experienced ostrich-hunters, and had made arrangements to proceed southwards on horseback in their company, while Lady Ettrick went on in the yacht to the Falkland Islands with the remainder of the *Firefly's* party, with the exception of Maeva and Colonel St. Leger Slade, who were to accompany Lord Ettrick. All the mids on board the *Dauntless* had had leave granted them by twos in turn ; and, in expectation of the coming Patagonian expedition, both Ronald and Esca had been able to arrange to come last on the list, and thus to obtain leave of absence for the trip. They had been ordered to rejoin the *Dauntless* at Santa Cruz, and the *Firefly*, moreover, was to pick up the others at the same place.

Two compelling forces were at work

within Maeva when she planned and obtained her father's consent to this expedition. The first was the desire to become acquainted with the lonely, far-stretching pampas, about which she and Lord Wrathness had so often talked at Ettrick Castle; and the other was a vague, undefinable feeling, that a fateful star might bring him across her path in this great lone land. How she yearned to see him again, hear his voice, and tell him in how far she knew his secret, and what up till then she had been able to effect in his favour, none could tell but herself. She longed with a passionate longing to see him again; she knew this well, and rejoiced that at least she had the opportunity given her of finding him if possible.

The ostrich-hunters had advised that
the expedition should strike rapidly into
the interior from El Carmen, through the
Travesia or desert; cross the Valchita
river and range of mountains of that
name; and traverse the Salinas, or salt-
infested lake territory, in the direction of
Lake Nahuelhuapi, at the base of the
Cordilleras Mountains of the Andes, in
the north-western portion of the country.
Hence they suggested a route southwards
to the Rio Chico, along whose banks a
straight run in could be made for Santa
Cruz. This line of march, they assured
Lord Ettrick, passed through a country
abounding in game, which would afford
not only sport, but the more necessitous
assurance of food. The route was, there-

fore, agreed upon. A start was made
with fifty horses, ten dogs, and three
guides, head of which François Delacroix,
already introduced to the reader, reigned
supreme.

This deviation in the way of explanation has led us from the scene of the
ostrich-hunt. So we must hark back to
where the break occurred, and take up
the thread of the story.

The pace at which the stalwart bird
had been proceeding, had begun to tell
upon its staying powers, and soon its
neck, which it had hitherto held out-
stretched in front of it, began to sink
lower, while there was a tremulous motion
apparent in its short wings, as though
it were seeking assistance to speed on

its flight from that quarter. All this the keen eye of François noted full well, and it encouraged him to renewed exertion. Spurring his horse onwards, he uttered a peculiar cry, one that was fully understood and appreciated by the hounds, judging by the spurt they put on, and the way in which they pulled themselves together. Flap, flap went the ostrich's wings—nearer and nearer crept up the hounds ; they were gaining now at every stride, La Plata still leading, La Liona lying next, Sultan bringing up the rear.

Suddenly, with a rush, the great black dog came up alongside the bird. " He has him ! " shouted Ronald, who was half mad with excitement, spurring his horse so as to be in at the death.

" Not a bit of it," shouted back Esca
who was equally excited, as with a rapid
movement the ostrich doubled to the left,
leaving La Plata to shoot ahead some
forty paces ere he could recover himself,
and speed on after the retreating and still
fast-fleeting quarry. But this movement
had given La Liona the advantage in
lead, and the game bitch did not throw
away her chance. Racing up to the
ostrich's stern, she grabbed savagely at
the thick grey tail that hung so temptingly
near her jaws. A cloud of feathers came
away in her mouth, half choking her and
impeding her action. The ostrich had
doubled again, but in doing so had almost rushed on instant death, for La
Plata faced him as he did so. With a

wriggle and a struggle, the plucky bird managed to evade him and sped onwards, but his pace decreased visibly, and both the dog and bitch had crept up on either side of him. For a time, by super-human exertions, constant doublings and twistings, he kept clear of them; but nature succumbed at length. With a spring the black dog had him by the throat, La Liona grabbed him by the back. Over and over the three rolled together, to be quickly joined by Sultan, who had come up in the rear, having tailed considerably the moment the pace began to tell; and soon nothing but a struggling heap of feathers and worrying dogs could be distinguished, amidst which the hunters rode up. Like lightning

François was off his horse and beating away the hounds with his whip ; then he seized the ostrich and broke its neck.

By this time the two midshipmen and Maeva had dismounted and clustered round the dead bird, which they examined closely. It was a fine, big specimen, well plumaged, and of a rich dark grey colour ; and as they discussed its appearance and the good run it had given them, François promised them a fat picane for dinner.

" Picane ! mais qu'est-ce que c'est que celà, François," inquired Ronald.

" Ah ! mais, monsieur, milord je veux dire, verra tout de suite, c'est un plat excellent, une viande dont la chaire en est succulente."

Ronald smacked his lips.

"Hurrah! Maeva," he cried, "we are
going to have a dish *par excellence* to-
night. Don't you feel hungry already
in anticipation?"

"You greedy!" she laughed, as she
playfully tried to box his ear. He jumped
on one side, but as he did so his face
became suddenly grave, and he pointed
with his whip over François' shoulder.
This latter was busy grollicking the
ostrich and tying it together, so he did
not perceive that which had arrested the
young earl's attention.

"Look, Esca!" exclaimed this latter.

Both Maeva and Esca looked in the
direction pointed out,—the wind was
blowing pretty sharply,—and they beheld
bearing down upon them a great bank

of dark, rolling smoke, from out of which forked tongues of fire were shooting heavenwards.

" Fire ! " shouted Esca, springing to his horse's head, a movement in which he was quickly imitated by Maeva and Ronald, the former taking care to secure the ostrich-hunter's as well. " François, voyez vous celà ? "

" Mon Dieu ! " ejaculated this latter, as he looked up on hearing Esca's question, and rapidly moved towards his horse. " Mais montez vite, bien vite."

In less time than it takes to tell it, all four were in the saddle, and the ostrich left lying where it was, forgotten.

" Ce sont les Indiens qui ont fait celà," said the Frenchman angrily, and

then he pointed out to the girl and
boys how the fire had got completely
between them and the remainder of their
party, whom they had left hunting more
to the southward. He next explained
in a few hurried words the position in
which they found themselves, and declared
that with horses tired by such a bursting
as theirs had just experienced, it would be
hopeless to try and race the flames. He
concluded by assuring them that there
was but one other alternative, and that was
to face the bank of smoke and ride through
it. He advised this latter course.

Ronald looked at Maeva and Esca.

"Are you game to try it?" he said,
inquiringly. "There is no time to be
lost, we must decide at once."

"Yes," they both assented, quickly. Esca was very pale. He had no fear for himself, his one thought was for Maeva. "O God! if anything should happen to her," he muttered to himself.

But François was speaking again, and to him they lent attentive ear. He had taken off his poncho, a thick woollen rug with a hole in the centre for the head to go through, and was winding it about his neck. He instructed them to do the same by theirs, for fortunately they were each provided with one of these garments. They quickly did as he bid them, and then he showed them how to wrap the ponchos round their faces in such a manner as to prevent the smoke from penetrating and stifling them; and finally he gave his last instructions. They were to ride as near the fire as they could, then wrap up their heads, stick their spurs into their horses, and charge with all their might. By good luck the pace would carry them through, but it was not a question or possibility of helping one another, it was a case in which the saying, " Every man for himself," held good.

" Let's stick together, Maeva," said Ronald, a little anxiously; "good heavens! if anything happened to you, what would mother say, and what should I do?"

Esca said nothing, but his large blue eyes were fixed on the girl with a look in which tender yearning and fear for her safety commingled.

Maeva caught the expression, and smiled.

"Think about yourselves, young men, and never mind me; why should I come to any more harm than you? After all, it's not in our hands at all. The matter lies with God."

They were all four riding abreast as she spoke, and the fire was bearing down upon them at a rapid pace; they could feel its heat upon their cheeks, and hear the savage crackle of the flames. François reined up.

"Maintenant!" he called out, "dépêchez-vous, messieurs et milady, protegez vos visages et en avant."

They did as he bid them, and at a signal from the ostrich-hunter stuck their

spurs into their horses' sides and pressed
them forward at full gallop. The thunder
of their rattling hoofs sounded across the
plain ; another minute and François, Ronald,
and Esca, closely followed by the dogs,
had dashed into the smoke and disappeared from view.

Not so Maeva. The horse which she
was riding was somewhat restive. As it
approached the flames it became terror-
stricken, and when she tried to urge it
forward, reared straight up in the air,
fought for a minute with its forefeet, and
then, wheeling round, dashed away in the
direction whence it had just come.

Hastily unwinding the poncho from
around her face, the girl slipped her
head through it and at once took in

the situation. To attempt to force her horse into the flames she saw would be impossible; and even if she had been minded to try again, he had settled the question by taking the bit between his teeth and tearing along at a headlong pace. She at once perceived that this was the very best course he could take, for the ground they were going over was covered with long, waving, dried-up grass, which acted like tinder on the flames, and increased their fury and dimensions every moment. Away to her left hand lay the Cordilleras. If she could but reach them in time she knew that she would be safe. But was this possible? As Maeva looked behind her and saw the dark column rushing on

like a whirlwind, she felt that nothing
but the mercy of God could intervene
between her and a terrible death.

"Oh! mother, dear mother,—Harold,
Ronald, Esca, if it were not for you I
would not mind; but, O God! for their
sakes help me to live," she cried out aloud,
as she dashed along. Maeva, we know,
was no coward, but it seemed hard to be
cut off from those she loved so dearly, and
at a moment too when the child believed
she was engaged on a work of mercy and
justice.

It soon became apparent that the horse's
speed was slackening fast, while the hot,
burning dust that showered around her,
told of the rapidly nearing flames. The
girl knew, that to urge the horse beyond

its powers, would merely result in bringing it to a standstill sooner than otherwise, for Maeva was no novice in the art of riding. It was second nature to her. She left the animal to itself, therefore, merely endeavouring to guide it as much as possible westward, by pressing the right rein on the right neck, and the poor beast answered to her call this time docilely enough, for fatigue was beginning to assert its sway over even the potent master, Fear.

They had breasted a tiny hill, from which she could perceive the flames creeping swiftly along like a huge snake westward to the mountains, enveloping the country all around, far as the eye could reach, in one vast sea of smoke and blackness.

The heat was oppressive, her tongue was dry and parched, her lips cracked and painful, her throat like parchment ; ah what in that moment would she not have given for a draught of water ?

Slower and slower went the horse ; its staying powers were vanishing fast, its movements grew feebler and feebler. Suddenly it broke into a trot, in another minute it was walking, then it halted, stopped dead short, rocked to and fro, and as Maeva threw herself from its back fell prone upon the ground.

" Poor horse,—poor, poor brute ! " the girl cried, as she knelt beside it and saw its eye glazing fast. " Oh for a drop of water to give you, and so ease the torture you must be enduring ! " She stopped short ; the horse was stiffening itself, a hot blast blew upon her cheek, the flames were shooting upwards, the fire was indeed upon her.

She sprang up and fled away before them like a startled deer. Fleet of foot and active of limb, yet, nevertheless, Maeva appeared to herself to be crawling along, in icomparison with those shooting, angry flames. Another hill rose before her, she breasted it rapidly ; her breath came thick and fast, she felt that she must choke, for the air was charged with nothing but dust and heat, and it well-nigh overpowered her.

As she rose to the hill's summit she looked ahead, despairingly expecting to see before her another wide tract of waving, dried-up grass. What was her surprise and joy to perceive a broad expanse of green reeds not half a mile away! and nestling amidst those reeds, on a slightly elevated piece of bushy ground, stood two canvas tents.

She strove to shout, but her throat refused the office; she could only utter a silent prayer as, encouraged by the sight before her, she put on a final spurt.

Evidently she had been perceived from the tents, for in a few minutes, though her eyes were glazed and filmy, she caught sight of a mounted horseman galloping to meet her. He came on at a rapid pace, and seemed to be urging his horse furiously in her direction; but this was all that Maeva made out, for at that moment she put her foot in a deep hole and, stumbling forward heavily and with a painful wrench, fell prone to the earth.

She could hear the fire behind her, the horse's hoofs in front of her, but the pain of her twisted ankle made her faint and giddy. The sky danced before her eyes, her brain seemed in a whirl. As she fell backwards with a low moan, the horse's hoofs rattled in her ear, and a voice broke in upon her last gleam of consciousness,—a voice which she could not mistake, which she knew only too well. Had it not haunted her day and night for many months gone by? and now with passionate eagerness she heard it exclaiming, as memory left her,—

" Maeva, my little darling ! O God ! can it be you—my love, my only love ? "

CHAPTER XIX

HE had sprung from his horse as he uttered that passionate cry. A man with a tall, graceful figure, and dark, dreamy, sad eyes. He lifted her from where she lay amidst the long, dry, waving grass, and pressed her to his heart with tender, respectful gentleness. She lay so still in his arms, the dark lashes falling on her pale, rigid cheeks, the sunny golden curls clustering about her high white forehead, that he could almost as he looked at her, with the hunger of a hopeless love in his eyes, have esteemed her dead. But he could not linger where he stood; already his horse was becoming restive with the heat and crackling of the hissing fire. Laying his precious burden across the saddle the man leaped up behind, and putting the animal into a gallop made straight for the green oasis in front of him.

He reached it quickly, and before the horse came to a standstill was on the ground.

"Guillaume!" he shouted, but the man was already in waiting with a hand on his master's bridle. As this latter tenderly lifted the child's still figure from the saddle and bore her to the nearest tent, the ostrich-hunter led the animal towards the centre of the green reeds, and having hobbled it, turned it loose among a troop of other horses. Then he went back towards the tent.

"Can I help the lord?" he inquired

in broken English, peering anxiously into the tent. Maeva was lying on a flattened heap of skins in one corner of it, and beside her knelt the dreamy, sad-eyed man who had rescued her by God's help from the jaws of death.

" Yes, Guillaume. Bring some water, quick," he answered huskily, as he knelt on by the motionless child's side, his right hand pressed against her heart, his left holding the small clenched fingers that had contracted together with pain as she fell to the ground. Oh! how his eyes devoured the fair white face, which he had thought never to see again, but which had haunted him in his dreams at night, his yearning thoughts by day, ever since that dark hour when, with the secret which had ruined his life, heavy upon him, he had stolen away from her presence with a terrible pain at his heart, which he felt could never pass away. And now, as lonely and companionless he roamed this vast un-explored land, a broken-hearted and weary man, this child, this love of his aching and saddened spirit, had come to cast one more gleam of happiness and hope into a life, that he had deemed fated never again to taste one spark of joy.

When the water came, he bade Guillaume get ready a fire and put some meat on for soup ; and as the man hurried off to obey his master's orders, he bent once more over the unconscious child.

Was it fancy, or did he dream it? She seemed to stir,—there was a flutter about the heart, a slight movement of the fingers. Gently he sprinkled a few drops of water on her forehead, and, while doing so, pushed back the golden curls that nestled thereon. As he did so he started, for across the ivory brow, running along parallel with the roots of the hair, stretched a long, blue, ugly-looking scar but recently healed, and presenting every appearance of having been incurred through violence. He passed his hand gently along this cruel-looking mark with an exclamation of pity. As he did so the child's eyelids unclosed, and the great grey eyes looked straight at him with wondering surprise. For a few minutes there was no sign of recognition apparent, but soon a light shone from them which there was no mistaking, for, where vacancy a minute hitherto had reigned, now joy and love had usurped their place.

She stretched out her hands towards him and smiled, the same glad, happy smile that he had often seen before ; he saw the warm flush of gladness rising to her cheeks, and noted how earnestly she regarded him ; with an uncontrollable impulse he bent over her, took the fair sweet face between his hands, and imprinted on her forehead one long, passionate kiss.

God help him! for he could not help himself. It was the act of a moment, the outburst of a heart that had suffered in lonely silence so long ; the craving of a love which, however irregular, existed, and could not be stifled at a moment's bidding. He did not pause to ask himself if that act was lawful or right; in that moment of happiness and intense joy he only knew one thing, and that was that the love of his lonely dreams was beside him once more, that the idol of his heart had come back to him again.

The blood rushed in a deep rich glow to her face; there was a mute appeal in her eyes, as though begging him not to try her too far; the bright drops welled up into them and ran over, but she brushed them hastily away as she looked through their glistening haze at him.

"Oh! Lord Wrathness, I am so glad it is you. I knew—I knew I should find you again if I came here, and now I have."

So she *had* thought of him when he was far away; she had not forgotten him altogether? His heart leapt for joy as he listened to the dear voice speaking, and noted the true-hearted ring it contained.

" Little friend," he said, tenderly, " did you think of your poor wandering acquaintance when he was far away? You did not quite forget him, then?"

" Forget *you?*" There was a ring of wonder in her voice, a simple, unaffected surprise which she did not attempt to conceal. " No," she added; " on the contrary, you have been ever in my thoughts."

His cup of happiness was brimful now. For a moment he forgot the weary past, with all its care, and trouble, and remorse. For a few brief, sweet moments he forgot the future, with all its dread anticipations and gloomy outlook. But this peaceful

oblivion did not last long, and memory
returned with bitter force to awaken it.

He started. How dared he kiss her as
he had? How dared he hold her hand as
he was doing? She, so true, so good, so
pure, so untainted by sin; while he, a
weary, world-tossed wanderer, tainted by
the commission of a terrible crime, linked by
a bond which only death could part, to a
bad, scheming, and revengeful woman, had
dared to act as he had.

"Child!" he cried, in a bitter, desperate
tone, "you should not be here. Where
did you come from?"

She shrank back from his touch, with a
terrible pain in her eyes. So he did not
care to see her?

"I could not help it," she answered,

gently. " It was the fire drove me this way, Lord Wrathness. We were ostrich-hunting, and it came on us suddenly. Ronald and Esca got through it, but my horse would not face it, and bolted. I left him dead on yonder hill, and hurried on before the flames. Then I saw you gallop-ing to meet me, and as I hurried faster I caught my foot in a touca-touca hole, and wrenched it badly, for I remember a dread-ful pain which made me feel faint and giddy. Then I remember hearing your voice, but after that nothing more."

He wondered if she had heard what he had said. Evidently not, or his last remark would not have hurt her so. He saw plainly that she was pained by it. In his heart he wondered if it would not be wiser

to let her keep this impression, but when
he pondered its advisability he felt that he
could not.   How could he drive her from
him with the thought that her presence
was distasteful to him, when he yearned to
tell her that it had brought him the first
moment of happiness which he had experienced for many and many a day?   He
could not do it.

"Little friend," he said, very gently,
"do not think I am not glad to see you.
Ah! my child, you have brought me
happiness too exquisite, too great, to last;
for weeks, for months, during my lonely
wanderings I have thought of you, and
the happy days we spent together before,
before——" he broke off abruptly.

"Did you get my letters?" he asked.

" Yes, Lord Wrathness," she replied. " I got them both, and I have got them still. I was very unhappy when I read them; first, because I could not understand why you had gone away so hurriedly. But I learnt it all soon afterwards, and then I understood."

His face turned ashen grey. He looked at her with a terrible earnestness.

" You learnt what? " he said, hoarsely.

" All about your trouble, your dreadful secret; all about what you have suffered and are suffering," she answered, in a low voice.

" My God! " he ejaculated, with a despairing gesture. " Who told you, child? "

" She did," she said, quietly. " Your wife, Lady Wrathness."

He sprang to his feet with a curse on his lips. So her vengeance had begun as she had threatened it would, and in a quarter, too, where she knew it would goad him most. He buried his face in his hands.

"Lord Wrathness," he heard the girl gently saying, "please don't be miserable about it. It will all come right some day. I never believed what she told me; you know in your letters you asked me not to believe all I heard, and I didn't. And though she hates you, and wants to make me hate you too, by blackening you in my eyes, she has failed entirely, for I know —I know you are innocent."

He groaned with anguish. He could not bear to deceive her. She believed

him innocent, and yet he stood before her
the murderer of his cousin. Had he
courage to tell her ?

"She came to see me," continued Maeva,
in the same gentle voice, "and tried to
find out from me where you had gone. I
did not know, and I told her so ; but
even if I had known I would not have
told her ; and then she told me those
wicked lies about you, and charged you
before me with murder. I was half mad ;
I sprang at her to deny it ; she struck
at me with her clenched fist. I remember
seeing her knuckles ringed with brass, and
I felt the blow strike me with fearful
violence ; but I remember no more. When
I came to I was on my bed, with mother,
and father, and Ronald, and the doctors

round me. It was but a brief consciousness, for I swooned again, and they told
me I laid for days before I came to and
rallied."

" Then it was she who gave you that
cruel scar ? " he asked fiercely, pointing to
her forehead.

" Yes, Lord Wrathness, it was she."

He ground his teeth. " The fiend !" he
exclaimed ; " did they arrest her ?"

" No, Lord Wrathness. I never would
tell any one about her, or who she was.
If I had, she would have told them that
dreadful story which she told me about
you."

" Staunch, true little friend !" he exclaimed, as the practical devotion of the
act presented itself forcibly to his mind.

"Ah! Lady Maeva, I don't suppose there's another like you in the world."

"I've got so much to tell you," she said, after a pause; "but, oh! Lord Wrathness, how am I to pass word to my father of my safety? My horse is dead, and I don't know the way. Can you help me?"

He started. He had been so wrapped up in seeing and talking to her again that he had never thought of asking her who she was with or anything about it. But now he recollected.

"The fire has burnt past my island," he answered, "and wherever it has passed will be a black, charred-up desert. You could never find your way, and God knows where they are at this moment.

But I have a man here who next to François Delacroix knows the pampas as well as I do Bond Street. I will send him to search for them, and to let them know you are safe. If any one will find them he will."

"Oh, thank you, thank you so much," she said, gratefully. "If they can only hear I am safe it will be a great relief to them, for I know by now they will be terribly anxious. That is to say if Ronald and Esca are safe. Oh! do you think they will have got through the fire all right?"

There was an anxious look in her eyes as she spoke. For the first time it struck her that they might not have succeeded in getting through that dense volume of smoke. She searched his face for an en-couraging reply.

" I have no doubt they are all right," he replied quickly, as he noticed her startled look. " I have ridden through pampas fires in the same way myself before. On horseback it can be done with a minimum of risk, if the animal can only be got to face the smoke, but on foot it would be impossible. However, I will go and send off Guillaume at once, and I feel sure he will find them for you ; so make your mind easy, and try and snatch a little rest till I return."

She lay back as he had bidden her and closed her eyes when he left the tent. Was it a dream ? Could it be reality ? Over and over again she asked herself the

question. Though she had hoped, trusted,
prayed to come across him in her wanderings, now that they had met she could
scarcely realize it as a fact. And yet it
must be true. Had she not heard his
voice, seen him again, felt the kindly clasp
of his hand, looked into those dear, sad
eyes of his, and felt the passionate, loving
kiss upon her forehead ? Wonderful as it
all seemed, Maeva felt it was no dream,
but really and absolutely true.

" Thank God ! " she whispered to herself,
and a happy smile played about her lips.
" So far all has gone well. If I can only
get that paper from that woman and de-
stroy it, he will be safe from her vengeance and can afford to defy her."

He had entered while she was thus

soliloquising to herself, but so gently that she did not hear him. ·Her eyes were still closed, and he stood by her side looking down on her childish, youthful face. He thought she had fallen asleep, she lay so still, and was fearful of disturbing her; but it was not so, for suddenly unclosing her eyes she perceived him.

"So you are back?" she cried, gladly springing up; but the next moment she had fallen back with a low, suppressed cry of pain. In an instant he was on his knees beside her.

"It is my ankle," she hastened to explain; "I fear I have wrenched it badly, for it is agony to stand on it. What a bore!" she continued in a troubled tone, "for I shall be a cripple for some time to come."

"Like I was," he said with a smile.

"Ah! no, not so bad as you were, Lord Wrathness," she replied, quickly. "After all, this is only a wrench or sprain; yours were terrible injuries,—and to think of it, too, I have never asked you how you were in regard to them."

"I—oh! I am all right again now," he said, quickly, "but something must be done for your foot. I have some Jacob's Oil fortunately, there is nothing like that for a sprain; it must be rubbed well into the foot, which must afterwards be securely bandaged. Thank goodness, I am a bit of a doctor and surgeon combined, and have all those things by me. I brought them from the yacht, as I never go into the wilds without them. But, first of all, that top boot of yours will have to be cut open. I can see how your poor foot has swollen into it; you would never be able to pull it off otherwise without intense pain and damage to the injured ankle."

She protested that it was a mere nothing, that it would pass away. But he knew better, and would take no denial. Very gently he ripped open the front part of the little brown-leather top-boot that encased the damaged foot, and then handed her the bottle and bandage. " Rub that well in," he said; "meanwhile, I will go and get you some soup, as Guillaume being gone in search of your party I am left to do cook's work in his absence. I daresay you will relish some soup, won't you ? "

"Thank you," she said, gratefully ; "how good and kind you are, and what trouble I am giving you ; nevertheless," she added, "it puts one in mind of old times, does it not? Only then you were the patient, I the nurse ; now you are the nurse and I the patient."

He laughed, almost lightly, if one who had suffered so much could be said to do so, as he left the tent once more.

The shades of evening were drawing on apace when he went outside, and the wind that had been blowing all day had sunk to rest. Far away on the distant horizon gleamed the blood-red, raging fire, still bent on its path of destruction ; and lighting up the darkening skies with a bright and lurid glare went the solid wall of flame which had brought him in the presence of Maeva, an unlooked-for and undreamed-of happiness.

He went over to the camp fire, which was burning merrily, the faithful Guillaume having piled it up before leaving, and examined the condition of the contents of the pot that was boiling thereon. Then he took a wooden spoon and tested the soup, which appeared to him satisfactory, for he nodded his head approvingly. After this he fetched a white enamelled tin bowl from the other tent, a small wooden spoon, and a little wooden jar with some salt in it, and having filled up the first-mentioned utensil with soup, took it over to Maeva's tent, where he found that she had finished rubbing and tying up her ankle. As gently as any nurse he put the soup beside her, raised her up, made her a soft back of guanaco skins against which to rest, and while she ate her soup busied himself putting the tent ship-shape, as he called it.

And, later on, when she had finished, he fastened the flaps of the tent open so that she could see outside. The camp fire gleamed and glimmered close at hand; above the sky was radiant in its pale moonlit beauty, the light from which lit up in silver sea-green radiance the pampas all around. A heavenly stillness had fallen upon them, broken only now and again by the muffled roar from some distant falling avalanche in the mighty Andes far away; and thus it was that Maeva and

Wrathness together looked upon that silent, lonely, strangely-mysterious land, about which he had so often told her in the early days of their acquaintance.

He had seated himself on the ground beside her low skin couch, and taken one of her tiny hands in his; and as they sat there together with the pale moonlight lighting up their faces, she told him all that she had done and dared for him since they had parted. She told him of Lady Wrathness's cruel, cold, and calculating letter, of how she had determined on discovering the truth. But here she paused. She dared not tell him of Richard Emerson's confession, or of the proofs of his (Wrathness's) innocence which Lady Wrathness held. Her oath to the

veritable murderer held her bound to
secrecy, and all she could tell the earl
was, that in so far as she had gone she
had discovered the existence of a plot
the unravelling of which could alone
establish his innocence.

And he, as he had listened to this
startling evidence of his non-participation
in a murder which for years he had been
led to believe he had committed, and
which had haunted him day and night
through all that time ; he, as he heard
from the lips of this brave, staunch girl-
friend of his, the glorious truth of his
innocence, felt a new life grow up within
him, a hope arising in his breast which
he had not dared hitherto to nurse. He
had risen from where he lay and knelt

beside her, and as her voice ceased speaking had taken both her hands in his. Bending over them he had kissed them tenderly, passionately, but with a deep and holy reverence; for was not this mere child not only the *first true* love of his life but his saviour from despair as well?

"Little friend!" he cried as he knelt beside her, "ah! more to me than all the world,—dear, kind, generous little friend, you have saved me from the most terrible of all dooms, Despair. Great God! I thank thee. Then I am not a murderer? I thank Thee, God."

CHAPTER XX.

AND while Maeva and Wrathness sat talking in the pale moonlight of the glad tidings she had brought him, far away to the westward, amidst the ruins of the blackened pampas, a lonely horseman rode silently and slowly along. Anon he would rein up and peer anxiously around him, only to pursue again his slow and silent course. Every now and then a deep groan or passionate sob would escape him, otherwise silence, blank, dead silence reigned around.

The moon shone down upon the horse

and its rider; the horse's head hung low, foam studded its mouth, from which the tongue hung limp and colourless; its movements were slow and laboured, as though its strength was well-nigh exhausted; ever and again it stumbled heavily.

" Poor brute! it is a shame to ride you," exclaimed the rider, as he dismounted and slackened the girths, and loosened the leathern strap which confined the wooden bit in the horse's mouth. " Poor brute! you are well-nigh done for, I fear, as indeed I hope I shall be too unless I find her. Oh! Maeva, my darling, my darling, where are you?"

His face was well in the moonlight as he spoke. It was the face of a handsome, noble-featured boy. He had no cap on his head, and the curls that clustered on his forehead shone bright beneath the silver streaks of light that fell upon them.   But his features were drawn with anxiety, and a haunting fear was in his eyes as they searched the blackened pampas all around.

The reader will have no difficulty in recognising Esca, or guessing upon what errand and quest he was bent.

When he and Ronald, François Delacroix, and Maeva had charged the advancing column of fire and smoke, he had found himself suddenly enveloped in intense darkness, mingled with a singular oppressiveness. Muffled up as his head was in the folds of the woollen poncho, this latter sensation as well as the utter blackness could be well accounted for.   As he entered the dense wall of wreathing flame and smoke, however, he felt his horse stagger and sway to and fro as if overcome with a sudden faintness. He felt, moreover, that the animal he be-strode was sinking to the ground, and at the same time a fearful sense of suffocation oppressed him. Yielding to the sudden impulse of the moment, knowing nothing of the direction in which he was proceeding, he dug his spurs into the animal's side and urged it forward by every means in his power. He felt the poor brute steady itself as if for a final effort, dash forward, and then he felt himself falling downward with a sudden crash ; and the next moment he was rolling on the ground, his hands clutching the burning grass, his senses overpowered well-nigh by the intolerable smell of smoke, and the dust that penetrated to and choked his nostrils.

Springing to his feet, with hands out-stretched before him, as though feeling for the liberty and rescue that he sought, Esca rushed madly forward. An electric shock appeared to have struck him. He felt like one who having staggered under a terrible load, was suddenly relieved of it. His lungs, oppressed hitherto with a heavy and crushing weight, became miraculously delivered. He seemed to live and breathe again, where up till then he had struggled, as it seemed to him, in the agonies of death.

Feeble as he felt himself, his first impulse was to unwind from his head the stifling poncho that enveloped it, and to look anxiously around him. Eagerly his eyes sought the one figure which they never met. He could see Ronald clinging to his horse's neck as though utterly over-powered ; he could see François dismounted and loosening the girths of his saddle. He saw besides the ostrich-hunter the three dogs—La Plata, La Liona, and Sultan, standing at their master's heels ; but one figure he looked for, strained his eyes for, all in vain, and that figure was Maeva's.

The cruel, angry, and spluttering fire dashed onwards. In less time than it takes to tell, it disclosed to Esca's view the blackened and charred form of the horse which had sunk to the ground beneath him, overpowered by the heat and smoke.

Mad with fear, he strained his eyes to catch the first sign of what he dreaded every moment to behold, the corpse of all he loved most dearly on this earth, aye, even beyond that idol of his childhood's days—his mother.

But he never saw it. The angry flames rushed onward, but no sign of Maeva did they disclose. As they retreated he followed them. She was not there. Then he heard the voice of François. The French-man was explaining to monsieur, whose terrified agitation he could perceive, that the horse which milady rode, was a young one, and had never yet faced a prairie fire. It had doubtless taken fright and vanished before the roaring flames.

And Ronald, who knew his cousin well,

had sought to cheer Esca with the certainty of her safety. " I know Maeva better than any one else, Esca," he had said ; " she is equal to any emergency. Ten to one her horse took fright. She let it have its course, and made up her mind to race the flaming prairie. Take my word for it, old boy, Maeva is safe. Often as children we have read about and discussed a prairie fire, and Maeva always told me that she would like nothing better than to be racing one. I give you my word of honour our darling old Maeva is safe."

But Esca would not be comforted. " Do you, Ronald, go on and tell Lord Ettrick. For myself I intend to look for her," he had answered. There was a pathetic ring

in his voice; and Ronald, who was Esca's
junior in the navy by twelve months, and
whom discipline had taught to obey, yielded
without demur.

When François learnt the young officer's
decision he at once offered him his horse.

"Nous ne sommes pas loin de Monsieur
le Marquis," he had protested; "et pour moi,
je puis aller à pied aussi bien qu'à cheval,
monsieur.   Ce n'est pas la première fois."

The offer was accepted.   Esca felt that if
Maeva had raced the prairie fire she would
be far from the spot where he stood, and
that therefore a horse was an absolute
necessity if he expected to come up with
her.   He had bidden his brother-mid a
quiet farewell, and desired him to make
all speed in rejoining Lord Ettrick, so that

the services of the ostrich-hunters might be quickly available in the search, which he felt sure would be instantly instituted, for Maeva. As for himself, he was so tortured with anxiety on her account, so oppressed with the fear that she needed assistance, that although he hardly knew in which direction he was going he felt that action alone could satisfy the craving at work within him, to find her and to help her.

Thus he had ridden all that weary afternoon. Wherever his eyes turned, blackened pampas met his gaze. He had pointed his horse's head for the first line of hills debouching on the Cordilleras. They were rocky and scant of herbage, and he knew that there the fire would burn itself out, and a wistful hope was in him that thither Maeva had fled for refuge, and that there he should come upon her. As he rode along he found himself picturing their meeting ; he could see in fancy the face of delight with which she would greet him ; he hoped and prayed that this evidence of his love would not be lost upon her, that at least she would know how dear to him was her comfort and safety.

And he had reached the hills at last, and riding to many of their highest summits had strained his eyes the black horizon round, hoping against hope to catch a sight of her of whom he was in search. In vain. Evening came on, darkness began to settle down, only far away the lurid glare of the vanishing fire lit up the distant horizon, but no sign of Maeva did he see. Long and loudly he shouted, but his voice came back to him alone in fading echoes until it grew hoarse and strained, and he could shout no more. His horse, too, was growing weary, and stumbled mechanically along; and thus it was that Esca had dismounted, having wandered into the plains again, and as he did so uttered the bitter cry for his friend and vanished love already related. He had tasted nothing since the early morning, but he did not feel hungry. Only now a thirst was beginning to parch his throat and make him long for water. The dust from the burnt-up prairie accelerated this desire, and had acted in a similar manner on the horse, whose sufferings have been but lately described. He could bear suffering, hardship, discomfort, could Esca Hamilton. His mother had always brought him up to be hardy and independent. She had impressed upon him the necessity for self-denial and self-sacrifice, knowing that his future life would in all probability be one of buffet and storm. In this moment of trial Esca was a living witness of the wisdom of that mother's care and devotion,—he was being tried and not found wanting.

" Poor brute!" he said again, as he stroked the horse's drooping neck. " You have done your best for me to-day, my poor fellow, and I wish I could get you some water; perhaps," he added, as a bright thought struck him. " if I give you your head, old man, you will find it for yourself."

As he spoke, he had taken the wooden bit entirely out of the animal's mouth, and fastening the leathern thong which acted as bridle loosely round its neck, had turned the horse adrift to go whither it pleased. For one second the poor beast paused, as if uncertain what to do; the next moment, however, it had set forward in a due easterly direction, at a brisker pace than hitherto, Esca keeping up alongside with his right hand resting on its withers.

It was the best course he could have adopted under the circumstances, for the sagacity of a horse in finding water is hardly equalled by any other animal, the camel alone excepted. Esca knew this, and, moreover, he was allowing hope to come to his rescue again, for he had just a glimmer of it in his heart, that the animal was making for some distant lake, and that perchance if this were so he should find Maeva there. Hope is a sweet thing. It buoys up the weariest heart, it assists the most physically tired, to renewed exertion.

The hours flew by, and still they tramped wearily on. The want of food, the burning desire for water, the long tiring day, the weary midnight tramp, were beginning to tell with cruel effect on the gallant-hearted boy.

To those who have never known what it is to find themselves alone on a great desert waste, foodless, waterless, friendless, with no knowledge of the country they are in, with nothing but wave after wave of land stretching away to the far horizon, will find it hard to realise the situation which this boy, hardly seventeen, had to face, or the position in which he found himself. A faint-hearted lad would have shrunk before the misery of the situation; would have knuckled under to the hopelessness of his lot. Not so Esca. The boy was born of plucky blood. His father in life had been plucky, his mother was made of that stuff, which can face both moral and physical suffering with heroism and calm fortitude. Was it likely that a child, born of such parents, would give in until such time as nature, strong even in the wealth of youth and health, succumbed?

He did not give in, but battled with himself, and toiled bravely on. His feet, blistered and aching, strove to keep pace with the almost as weary horse. His eyes, half closed with fatigue and prostration, struggled to keep open and to look ahead. His store of hope, sinking almost to extinction, he strove to keep alight. This is what buoyed him up,—the thought that if he held on he should find Maeva.

On, on they toiled. Dawn was beginning to break in the pale horizon. The moon, high in the heavens, shone down upon the yellow curly head of the sinking boy. Nature was failing fast now, for thirst, that terrible demon, that most awful of tortures, had taken possession of the wiry, athletic frame. Against its potency and strength none can battle. It strikes the strongest down.

He was hanging to the saddle now. His head had sunk upon his chest in apathetic lethargy. Mechanically his legs moved, but all around was dark. He felt nothing, saw nothing, noticed nothing ahead or around. Suddenly the weary horse pricked up its ears and neighed. An answering neigh came back. The animal quickened its pace, started forward into a broken trot, increased it to a laboured gallop, and was gone. In a few minutes it had entered a reedy, marshy locality, and had buried its nose to the eyes in a clear cool pool of water, while around it stamped and neighed a troop of some twenty horses,

And Esca, where was he? On the

threshold of relief, within a hundred paces of rescue, not two hundred yards away from where Maeva lay peacefully sleeping, the boy had fallen when the horse dashed forward,—fallen to the ground speechless, helpless, senseless, in a dying state, uncared for, unthought of, and alone.

END OF VOL. II.

Printed by Hazell, Watson, & Viney, Ld., London and Aylesbury.

www.ingramcontent.com/pod-product-compliance
Lightning Source LLC
Chambersburg PA
CBHW020057030726
47498CB00006B/1825